APULEIUS

The Tale of
Cupid and Psyche

APULEIUS

The Tale of Cupid and Psyche

Translated, with Prefaces, Allegorical Appendices, Afterthoughts, and Index, by

Joel C. Relihan

Hackett Publishing Company, Inc.
Indianapolis/Cambridge

14 13 12 11 10 09   1 2 3 4 5 6 7

For further information, please address
  Hackett Publishing Company, Inc.
  P.O. Box 44937
  Indianapolis, Indiana 46244-0937

  www.hackettpublishing.com

Cover design by Abigail Coyle
Interior design by Elizabeth L. Wilson
Composition by Professional Book Compositors, Inc.
Printed at Versa Press, Inc.

Library of Congress Cataloging-in-Publication Data

Apuleius.
    [Psyche et Cupido. English]
    The tale of Cupid and Psyche / Apuleius ; translated, with prefaces, allegorical appendices, afterthoughts, and index, by Joel C. Relihan.
        p. cm.
    Includes bibliographical references and index.
    ISBN 978-0-87220-972-5 (pbk.) — ISBN 978-0-87220-973-2 (cloth)
    1. Psyche (Greek deity)—Fiction. 2. Eros (Greek deity)—Fiction.
I. Relihan, Joel C. II. Title.
    PA6209.M5R45 2009
    873′.01—dc22   2008043299

∞

For Elise

as always

τῇ ψυχῇ τῆς ψυχῆς μου

Contents

About This Edition

The tale of *Cupid and Psyche* is one of a number of stories inserted by Apuleius into his Latin *Metamorphoses*, better known as *The Golden Ass*. The term "inserted" is appropriate because there is a much briefer, much plainer, much more uniform Greek version of this story of a man turned into an ass that clearly reflects Apuleius' model in outline for the pull-out-all-the-stops extravagance of his profligate romance (I avoid the term "novel," though many prefer it). *Cupid and Psyche* is the longest and most elaborate of these inserted tales and is fully capable of standing on its own. Yet modern critical opinion is united in claiming that *Cupid and Psyche* has been carefully adapted, in structures, themes, and details, to fit into the fabric of the whole of *The Golden Ass*. As a tale of curiosity with disastrous consequences, of punishment, wandering, and redemption, it is a crucial parallel to the story of the narrator himself. The readers of the whole realize when they get to Storisend (to borrow a name from *Jurgen*) that the epiphany of Isis and the return of the redeemed ass to his human shape have been well prepared for. Consequently, when *Cupid and Psyche* is excerpted as it is in this English edition, it is necessarily presented without its context, and one could say that violence has been done to it. Yet its broad fame and lively influence in the Western literary tradition derive primarily from its status as a fiction independent of its source. By presenting it in isolation, I seek to facilitate an appreciation of this fame and influence and to make it easier to ask the question, *Just what is this story that has been bent to Apuleius' larger purposes*?

This is a golden moment in Apuleian studies. The crown of the Groningen Commentaries on Apuleius has finally arrived in the form of a 600-page commentary on *Cupid and Psyche* (Zimmerman et al. 2004).[1] Further, two studies on Apuleius and his

---

1. A further Groningen commentary has been promised for Book 11, to replace the 1975 commentary of J. Gwyn Griffiths.

influence have just appeared, practically simultaneously: Robert H. F. Carver, *The Protean Ass: The* Metamorphoses *of Apuleius from Antiquity to the Renaissance* (2007) and Julia Haig Gaisser, *The Fortunes of Apuleius and the* Golden Ass: *A Study in Transmission and Reception* (2008). The artistic influence of *Cupid and Psyche* is fully documented in Sonia Cavicchioli's *The Tale of Cupid and Psyche: An Illustrated History* (2002); and Jan M. Ziolkowski's *Fairy Tales from Before Fairy Tales: The Medieval Latin Past of Wonderful Lies* (2007), though not dealing with *Cupid and Psyche* specifically, may be consulted with profit concerning *The Donkey Tale*.[2] These books sum up much of the voluminous literature concerning Apuleius and this story and constitute the necessary starting points, along with the annotated bibliography of Schlam and Finkelpearl (2000), itself now supplemented in Zimmerman et al. (2004, pp. 570–76), for any serious further study. This edition cannot and does not attempt to replicate these crucial works, nor does it attempt to provide any sort of thorough bibliographical orientation to Apuleius or *The Golden Ass*; rather, it hopes to encourage a diverse readership to a fresh contemplation of the complexities of the story. For, in fact, appreciations of its relevance to the frame story of the adventures of Lucius, the man-turned-ass, have at times glossed over the difficulties of the story per se. Thus, for the mythology student investigating the lore surrounding Venus and Cupid; for the folklore student with an eye on the Mysterious Husband, the Violated Prohibition, or Psyche's Cinderella-like tasks; for the art student investigating the Renaissance painting cycles of Rafael or Giulio Romano; for the psychology student pondering a Freudian tale of sexual development or a Jungian account of individuation or perhaps even the distant origins of the discipline of psychology itself; for the philosophy student looking at a Platonic allegory concerning the soul; for the student of literature or religion tracing a line from Apuleius to C. S. Lewis, this edition focuses on a single story; how the story relates to all the other stories of *The Golden Ass* readers may pursue on their own.

---

2. The clear *desiderandum* in Apuleian studies now is a thorough monograph on the history of *Cupid and Psyche* in modern literature: Keats, William Morris, Robert Bridges, *Beauty and the Beast*, Couperus' *Psyche*, Lewis' *Till We Have Faces*. Accardo 2002 is a start.

The text is taken directly from my translation of the entire *Golden Ass* (Relihan 2007, pp. 83–128).[3] I have included a little bit on either side of the story, not to relate it to Lucius' story so much as to introduce the young woman to whom this story is told (the narrator of *The Golden Ass* only overhears it) and to bring to a conclusion the story of the old woman who narrates it, for every story must have a listener and a teller. The running heads of the original translation have been removed here and, to present the tale as a continuous story, I have marked the book divisions—very important in the architecture of the romance as a whole (the story spans Books 4 to 6 of the original)—much more subtly. In place of the running heads, I have introduced a number of subtitles to mark the progress of the story; these too are purely authorial and are not deployed in order to indicate in themselves what may be the larger structures of the plot (i.e., whether it is a five-act drama or is tripartite or bipartite). The Reader's Commentary, available online, draws parallels, raises questions, underlines crucial points, and points out crucial inconsistencies; any reader inspired by this presentation of the tale to study it further will necessarily turn to Kenney's shorter edition and commentary of the Latin text of 1990 or to the massive commentary of Zimmerman et al. 2004.

The English of this translation represents an attempt to reflect the linguistic exuberance of the Latin original, inspired to employ its own alliterations, rhymes, archaisms, and anachronisms as best it can; these do not reflect the Apuleian original text in any sort of one-to-one correspondence, however. Style is part of meaning, and a blander or more sentimental English would obstruct what to my mind is one of the crucial aspects of the audience's reaction to the original: *Surely this is too much*! Verb tenses may seem erratic, as Apuleius generally uses past tenses for simple narration but switches to the present whenever there is the least bit of dramatic tension or narrative drive. Indirect speech is given an archaic flavor by being printed in italics. To the greatest

---

3. One correction and a few typographical changes have been made: at 6.23, Psyche is offered a goblet of ambrosia, not of nectar; at 5.6 and 5.18, *Yes* has been substituted in "nods yes" and "says *yes*"; at 6.7, *No* in "nod no"; at 4.29, 5.6, and 5.31, Venus' replaces Venus's; at 6.2, goddess' replaces goddess's; at 5.9, gemstones replaces gem stones.

extent possible, I have striven for consistency in the translation of key words and word roots and also of adverbs and transitional particles; the reappearance of such words is designed to remind the reader of previous appearances and so bind the words and the work together. The three appendixes, translations of fifth- and sixth-century accounts of what is felt to be the story's allegorical content, as well as an excerpt from Apuleius himself concerning the nature of Love as an intermediary spirit, reflect the translations of a few key terms from the Apuleius text (e.g., *curiositas* is not the neutral term "curiosity" but the "sticking one's nose in" that is used throughout *The Golden Ass*). I hope that the reader will find the consistency thus imposed upon the text and its allegorizations useful, if at times a little jarring.

But I have avoided writing a traditional introduction. *To the Reader* presents four crucial Platonic passages that a reader should have in mind before beginning the story: three on the wingèd nature of the Soul and its relation to Love from *Phaedrus* and one on the distinction between Heavenly Aphrodite and Vulgar Aphrodite from *Symposium*. Also given in outline there are details of the iconography of *Cupid and Psyche* as revealed in artwork prior to Apuleius' time, drawing primarily on the fundamental study by Carl Schlam in *Apuleius and the Monuments* (1976). A passage from Plotinus is also quoted, demonstrating that stories of Cupid and Psyche in various forms had a currency both in literary and in artistic media even after Apuleius' day. I think that a reader trying to make sense of the whole needs to be aware of these at the outset, as any ancient reader would have brought them to bear even if not aware of Apuleius' pretensions as a Platonic philosopher. The reader may then attack the work with a lively mind. The concluding Afterthoughts will offer a particular—and I will not say unbiased—way through its labyrinth that does take the *contrast* between *Cupid and Psyche* and its frame as a source of insight into what *Cupid and Psyche*'s particular objectives are.

My debts are few and pleasant to record. I first offer my deep thanks to Gregory Hays, the master of Fulgentian studies, who offered such useful comments on my translation from the *Mythologies* and allowed me to draw on parts of his forthcoming and magisterial commentary on Fulgentius. He will recognize his influence in more places than my notes could acknowledge. John Partridge, the master of the *daimonion* of Socrates, was a profound help in all matters concerning the first appendix, both as guide and as reader. I also thank my colleagues Grace Baron and David Wulff for being readers of the whole and for offering both their encouragement and their psychological insights. My daughter Clare was a most valuable proofreader. Ellen Finkelpearl read the final product with a discerning eye. My deepest debt is, again, recorded in the dedication.

Joel C. Relihan
Wheaton College
Norton, Massachusetts

To the Reader:
A Brief Prehistory
of *Cupid and Psyche*

Further proof that our good is in the realm above is the love innate in our souls; *hence the coupling in picture and story of Eros with Psyche*. The soul, different from the divinity but sprung from it, must needs love. When it is in the realm above, its love is heavenly; here below, only commonplace. The heavenly Aphrodite dwells in the realm above; here below, the vulgar, harlot Aphrodite.

Every soul is an Aphrodite, as is suggested in the myth of Aphrodite's birth at the same time as that of Eros. As long as soul stays true to itself, it loves the divinity and desires to be at one with it, as a daughter loves with a noble love a noble father. When, however, the soul has come down here to human birth, it exchanges (as if deceived by the false promises of an adulterous lover) its divine love for one that is mortal. And then, far from its begetter, the soul yields to all manner of excess.

But when the soul begins to hate its shame and puts away evil and makes its return, it finds its peace.
—Plotinus, *Enneads* VI 9 [9], 9, trans. E. O'Brien 1964, 85–6 (emphasis added)

The Greek Neoplatonic philosopher Plotinus (204–70) is writing here not quite a century after the Latin Middle Platonic philosopher Apuleius (125?–170?) wrote his *Metamorphoses,* the romance of which the present story *Cupid and Psyche* forms a large and enigmatic part. We do not imagine that either Plotinus or Porphyry, his student and editor, was aware of Apuleius. But what Plotinus here makes clear, and what the reader of Apuleius must be aware of, is that relations between Cupid and Psyche (or, in Greek, Eros and Psyche) were the stuff of both philosophical lore and popular art for at least 600 years before Apuleius put pen to paper.

There is no evidence that anything like Apuleius' tale of *Cupid and Psyche* existed in written form beforehand; while many details have their pedigrees, the whole is Apuleius' own. And Apuleius is a canny manipulator of stories and sources; whatever has gone into *Cupid and Psyche* has been modified to serve the demands of his art and his story. Consider the *Metamorphoses*, or *Golden Ass*, as a whole. As a tale of a man turned into a donkey, it is no doubt to be related to a folktale tradition, underground in Classical literature, that surfaces in the Middle Ages as the *Asinarius*, the tale of a man born an ass but who sheds that skin in consequence of the love of a woman who marries him. Yet Apuleius' tale, for all the sex of its beginning and for all the erotic details of the stories told along the way, has the ass regain his shape most chastely, eating roses provided by the goddess Isis, his protector and redeemer; sex is not a path to redemption, and marriage is not part of the story. In the Greek story *Onos* (*The Ass*), which is derived from what we are certain is the literary model for the outline of *The Golden Ass*, the narrator, once returned to his human shape, goes back to the woman who loved him as an ass only to find that she is no longer impressed with his merely human sexual proportions. In Apuleius, the transformed ass never even thinks about the matron who loved him but, as a devotee of Isis, goes to Rome to become a lawyer. In other words, the savvy reader is aware that Apuleius knows some traditions and subverts them; the reader is expecting one thing and is given another and evaluates accordingly. What I present here by way of preamble to the story (leaving traditional introductory material for the concluding "Afterthoughts") is what the ancient reader, or listener, would have brought to the story when encountering it for the first time.

Of course, it is not possible under the current circumstances to duplicate the experience of a first-time ancient reader or listener. Apuleius did not write anything labeled *Cupid and Psyche*; it is a story with no separate subheading, one told by a drunk old woman, the cook and slave to a band of robbers, to a young woman who has been abducted for ransom just before her wedding. One has no idea when it begins how long it will go on. The fact that you have in your hands a book called *Cupid and Psyche* with some fifty text pages devoted to the tale deprives you of much of the suspense that Apuleius as author tried to create for it. For example, he loves here as elsewhere to introduce characters and reveal names later. The story begins at section 4.28 with the introduction of the beautiful youngest daughter of an unnamed king and queen; at the end of 4.30 we are told her name, and we are supposed to be startled: *So this fairy tale is about Soul?* Cupid is introduced as a character early on, the son whom Venus enlists to punish this Psyche, but without a name, only as the boy with the wings and the arrows. This Cupid is not directly named, nor do we learn that Cupid is the name of Psyche's demon lover until 5.22, and though we have been building to this climax for quite a while, only the dullest reader would have been as surprised as Psyche is shown to be, for any reader would know that a love story with Psyche must be about Cupid as well. Then the story proceeds in Cupid's absence, with Venus in the role of tormentor. The reader is puzzled: *But doesn't Cupid lead Psyche to heaven? And aren't the tortures of Psyche supposed to be a part of Cupid's regimen? And is this Venus supposed to be the Heavenly Aphrodite?*

The reader needs some orientation in this complicated question of how to read a surprising mixture of fairy tale and philosophical allegory. Cupid and Psyche are elsewhere represented in various ways, and it is clear when Plato in *Phaedrus* has Socrates speak of the gooseflesh that a lover feels in the presence of his beloved as proof of the soul's preexisting wingèd nature, and of how Love serves as an intermediary to return the wingèd soul to the place of its origin, that he is playing with iconographic conventions established before his time. What Apuleius' reader knows, and the questions such knowledge may reasonably generate, I would list as follows:

1. Cupid with wings is frequently depicted with a woman with bird wings. But Psyche is often associated with a butterfly, and the first pairing of a bird-winged Cupid and a butterfly-winged Psyche is dated to around 300 BCE. A modern version of this pairing may be found on the cover of this volume. The reader needs to ask, *Does Apuleius' Psyche ever have wings, butterfly or otherwise?*

2. There is a symbolic relationship between the butterfly and the human soul: that which emerges from the body the way a butterfly emerges from a chrysalis. *Does Psyche rise up from this world, and is Cupid here an intermediary?*

3. A very common representation of the pair is in an embrace, often as just a sentimental, frankly kitschy, grouping. *Do we ever see the pair in an embrace in this tale?*

4. Cupid can be seen torturing Psyche; his traditional bow, arrow, and torch are the tools by which a soul may be put to the

test or purified. *Does Cupid ever have a torch here? Does Cupid actually torture Psyche?*

5. In a parallel tradition, Psyche can be seen torturing Eros, subjecting him to the torments to which lovers are traditionally subjected. This is more of a poetic than a philosophic tradition: Love Chastised. *Are there reflections of that tradition here?*

6. Cupid and Psyche can be seen in Dionysiac contexts, as attendants at the wedding of Dionysus and Ariadne. They are shown more often with Dionysus than with Aphrodite. *Does Dionysus show up here? And what would the wedding of Cupid and Psyche themselves mean in this context?*

7. They can be multiplied, various Cupids and Psyches going about various human activities associated with feasting or with marriage. But there is also the Platonic tradition of the two Aphrodites, Heavenly and Vulgar, as referred to by Plotinus above. There is much talk of multiple Venuses in *Cupid and Psyche. Can a case be made for multiple Cupids as well? And can the one Venus have her functions and appearances divided in two, now as those of the Heavenly, now as those of the Vulgar, Venus?*

8. Cupid and Psyche are found with increasing frequency on sarcophagi, both Christian and pagan, in the second century when Apuleius is writing. *Does this* Cupid and Psyche *assert the immortality of the soul, giving hope in the face of the reality of death? And if it speaks of the ascent of Soul, does it also speak of its descent into the world of matter, as seemed to Plotinus to be a crucial part of the Platonic account?*

9. Psyche can be found with a sleeping Cupid. This happens here too, in a literally spectacular way. *Is this part of an erotic account of how individuals relate to love, or is it part of the story of how Psyche finds her way to the immortal and unchanging world?*

10. The Platonic texts speak of a male soul being inspired by the beauty of a boy. *Is* Cupid and Psyche *as a love story between a woman and a man in and of itself a subversion of the allegorical account of the Human Soul (ψυχή or* anima, *grammatically feminine) and its relations with Divine Love (Ἔρως or Cupido, grammatically masculine)? What does it mean that Apuleius returns to the world of heterosexual love a story that Plato adapted in a pederastic context to speak of the superiority of nonprocreative love?*

Cupid and Psyche exists at the intersection of Platonic philosophy, folktale, and popular religion. Interpreting it is not a question of disentangling these threads but of coming to appreciate why they have been so braided together. The Platonic texts that must be understood will conclude this introduction. A few other furnishings of the ancient reader's mind must also be explained before the story is read. First, the original reader had already read the first three and a half books of *The Golden Ass* and therefore knew there was no attempt to characterize speakers by their language. The old woman uses the same language as the main narrator, so you need not ask how the old woman knows these Platonic concepts or why she speaks in such an artificial manner. But you are free to ask whether she is adapting her tale to the plight of the woman who is her audience, insofar as she understands that plight. Furthermore, the old woman is the only omniscient third person narrator in all of the romance. This narratological difference entitles you to wonder to what extent the old woman is just a stand-in for Apuleius himself or for Lucius himself. To put it another way, Lucius, the main narrator who was turned into an ass because of a mistake with a magic potion and who was abducted by robbers and brought to their cave just as the bride-to-be was, overhears this story. The author of the whole, who speaks the prologue of *The Golden Ass* and does not clearly indicate whether he is or is not Lucius the narrator, presents a story in which an ass records after the fact (he wasn't a stenographer, after all, as he admits at 6.25) what he overheard an old woman tell a bride. You may well ask: *Who vouches for the truth of all this?*

Four Platonic Texts

1. *Phaedrus* 246c, trans. Alexander Nehamas and Paul Woodruff in Cooper 1997, 524. [Socrates has been presenting the famous description of the soul as being like a charioteer with two winged horses, one beautiful and noble, the other base and recalcitrant.]

All soul looks after all that lacks a soul, and patrols all of heaven, taking different shapes at different times. So long as its wings are in perfect condition it flies high, and the entire universe is its dominion; but a soul that sheds its wings wanders until it lights on something solid, where it settles and takes on an earthly body, which then, owing to the power of the soul, seems to move itself. The whole combination of soul and body is called a living thing, or animal, and has the designation 'mortal' as well. Such a combination cannot be mortal, not on any reasonable account.

2. *Phaedrus* 248b–c, trans. Nehamas and Woodruff in Cooper 1997, 526. [The gods are able to see the place beyond heaven where true reality lies; mortal souls desire to see it but have difficulty.]

The reason there is so much eagerness to see the plain where truth stands is that this pasture has the grass that is the right food for the best part of the soul, and it is the nature of the wings that lift up the soul to be nourished by it. Besides, the law of Destiny is this: If any soul becomes a companion to a god and catches sight of any true thing, it will be unharmed until the next circuit; and if it is able to do this every time, it will always be safe. If, on the other hand, it does not see anything true because it could not keep up, and by some accident takes on a burden of forgetfulness and wrongdoing, then it is weighed down, sheds its wings and falls to earth.

3. *Phaedrus* 250d–252b, trans. Nehamas and Woodruff in Cooper 1997, 528–29. [Socrates speaks about the nature of the wingèd soul and how it tries to recall the beauty that it had observed in the truly real world, that it beheld in the company of the gods, prior to its descent into the body and the physical world.] •

Now beauty, as I said, was radiant among the other objects; and now that we have come down here we grasp it sparkling through the clearest of our senses. Vision, of course, is the sharpest of our bodily senses, although it does not see wisdom. It would awaken a terribly powerful love if an image of wisdom came through our sight as clearly as beauty does, and the same goes for the other objects of inspired love. But now beauty alone has this privilege, to be the most clearly visible and the most loved. Of course a man who was initiated long ago or who has become defiled is not to be moved abruptly from here to a vision of Beauty itself when he sees what we call beauty here; so instead of gazing at the latter reverently, he surrenders to pleasure and sets out in the manner of a four-footed beast, eager to make babies; and, wallowing in vice, he goes after unnatural pleasure too, without a trace of fear or shame. A recent initiate, however, one who has seen much in heaven—when he sees a godlike face or bodily form that has captured Beauty well, first he shudders and a fear comes over him like those he felt at the earlier time; then he gazes at him with the reverence due a god, and if he weren't afraid people would think him completely mad, he'd even sacrifice to his boy as if he were the image of a god. Once he has looked at him, his chill gives way to sweating and a high fever, because the stream of beauty that pours into him through his eyes warms him up and waters the growth of his wings. Meanwhile, the heat warms him and melts the places where the wings once grew, places that were long ago closed off with hard scabs to keep the sprouts from coming back; but as nourishment flows in, the feather shafts swell and rush to grow from their roots beneath every part of the soul (long ago, you see, the entire soul had wings). Now the whole soul seethes and throbs in this condition. Like a child whose teeth are just starting to grow in, and its gums are all aching and itching—that is exactly how the soul feels when it begins to grow wings. It swells up and aches and tingles as it grows them. But when it looks upon the beauty of the boy and takes in the stream of particles flowing into it from his beauty (that is why this is called "desire"), when it is watered and warmed by this, then all its pain subsides and is replaced by joy. When, however, it is separated from the boy and runs dry, then the openings of the passages in which the feathers grow are dried shut and keep the wings from sprouting. Then the stump of each feather is blocked in its desire and it throbs like a pulsing artery while the feather pricks at its passageway, with the result that the whole soul is stung all around, and the pain simply drives it wild—but then, when it remembers the boy in his beauty, it recovers its joy. From the outlandish mix of these two feelings—pain and joy—comes anguish and helpless ravings. In its madness the lover's soul cannot sleep at night or stay put by day; it rushes, yearning, wherever it expects to see the person who has that beauty. When it does see him, it opens the sluice-gates of desire and sets free the parts that were blocked up before. And now that the pain and the goading have stopped, it can catch its breath and once more suck in, for the moment, this sweetest of all pleasures. This it is not at all willing to give up, and no one is more important to it than the beautiful boy.

It forgets mother and brothers and friends entirely and doesn't care at all if it loses its wealth through neglect. And as for proper and decorous behavior, in which it used to take pride, the soul despises the whole business. Why, it is even willing to sleep like a slave, anywhere, as near to the object of its longing as it is allowed to get! That is because in addition to its reverence for one who has such beauty, the soul has discovered that the boy is the only doctor for all that terrible pain.

4. *Symposium* 180c–181d, trans. Nehamas and Woodruff in Cooper 1997, 465–66. [Apollodorus relates to his friend the speeches about the nature of Love given long ago at a symposium held at Agathon's house; he learned them from Aristodemus. Here, Apollodorus says that Aristodemus said that Pausanias began as follows after a speech by Phaedrus, the one to whom Socrates spoke about the soul and its wings in the dialogue named after him and quoted above.]

"Phaedrus (Pausanias began), I'm not quite sure our subject has been well defined. Our charge has been simple—to speak in praise of Love. This would have been fine if Love himself were simple too, but as a matter of fact, there are two kinds of Love. In view of this, it might be better to begin by making clear which kind of Love we are to praise. Let me therefore try to put our discussion back on the right track and explain which kind of Love ought to be praised. Then I shall give him the praise he deserves, as the god he is.

"It is a well-known fact that Love and Aphrodite are inseparable. If, therefore, Aphrodite were a single goddess, there could also be a single Love; but, since there are actually two goddesses of that name, there also are two kinds of Love. I don't expect you'll disagree with me about the two goddesses, will you? One is an older deity, the motherless daughter of Uranus, the god of heaven: she is known as Urania, or Heavenly Aphrodite. The other goddess is younger, the daughter of Zeus and Dione: her name is Pandemos, or Common Aphrodite. It follows, therefore, that there is a Common as well as a Heavenly Love, depending on which goddess is Love's partner. And although, of course, all the gods must be praised, we must still make an effort to keep these two gods apart.

"The reason for this applies in the same way to every type of action: considered in itself, no action is either good or bad, honorable or shameful. Take, for example, our own case. We had a choice between drinking, singing, or having a conversation. Now, in itself none of these is better than any other: how it comes out depends entirely on how it is performed. If it is done honorably and properly, it turns out to be honorable; if it is done improperly, it is disgraceful. And my point is that exactly this principle applies to being in love: Love is not in himself noble and worthy of praise; that depends on whether the sentiments he produces in us are themselves noble.

"Now the Common Aphrodite's Love is himself truly common. As such, he strikes wherever he gets the chance. This, of course, is the love felt by the vulgar, who are attached to women no less than to boys, to the body more than to the soul, and to the least intelligent partners, since all they care about is completing the sexual act. Whether they do it honorably or not is of no concern. That is why they do whatever comes their way, sometimes good, sometimes bad; and which one it is is incidental to their purpose. For the Love who moves them belongs to a much younger goddess, who, through her parentage, partakes of the nature both of the female and the male.

"Contrast this with the Love of the Heavenly Aphrodite. This goddess, whose descent is purely male (hence this love is for boys), is considerably older and therefore free from the lewdness of youth. That's why those who are inspired by her Love are attracted to the male: they find pleasure in what is by nature stronger and more intelligent. But, even within the group that is attracted to handsome boys, some are not moved purely by this Heavenly Love; those who are do not fall in love with little boys; they prefer older ones whose cheeks are showing the first traces of a beard—a sign that they have begun to form minds of their own. I am convinced that a man who falls in love with a young man of this age is generally prepared to share everything with the one he loves—he is eager, in fact, to spend the rest of his own life with him. He certainly does not aim to deceive him—to take advantage of him while he is still young and inexperienced and then, after exposing him to ridicule, to move quickly on to someone else."

The Tale of

Cupid and Psyche

being an excerpt from

the Latin romance

Metamorphoses

or

The Golden Ass

by the

Philosopher and Rhetorician

Apuleius
of
Madauros

The Audience Arrives

. . . The robbers came back just then, all beside themselves, in anxious caution out of all proportion; to be sure, they had with them absolutely nothing, not a single bundle or bale, not even a scrap of cloth, not even a cheap one, but for all their swords, for all their hands—no, more: for all the strength and force of their conspiracy—they brought with them nothing but a single, solitary maiden. She was well-born, a woman of quality, and, as her ladylike dress and demeanor indicated, from the upper social strata in these parts. She was a girl, believe you me, who could even win the love and desire of an ass like me, but full of sorrow and lamentation, ripping at her clothes and tearing at her hair. Hustling her inside the cave and trying at the same time to alleviate and assuage her anguish, they approach and address her in these words:

"Please, m'lady, rest assured of both your salvation and your honor, and just grant a little of your patience to our plan for our profit: it was the pressure of poverty that drove us to this sect. But your mother and your father, money-grubbing people though they may very well be, will for all that doubtless scrape together without delay from the high-piled heaps of their riches an appropriate price of redemption for their own flesh and blood."

This pointless palaver—more of the same followed it—allays the girl's anguish not one bit. It never stood a chance. She hung her head and let it rest between her knees, and so she wept without surcease. But the robbers called for the old woman, brought her inside, and told her to sit with the girl and to console her with what sympathetic approach and address she could; then they went into conference together, conducting their band's usual business. But for all that, despite all of the poor old woman's attempts and arguments, the girl could not be talked out of the tears that had already begun to flow; in fact, wailing and bewailing herself from deep down within and wracking herself in abdominal convulsions with incessant sobbing, she even made the tears start from my own eyes.

Yet this was her reply: "How could I," she said, "victim that I am!—in solitary exile from such a home, from a household of such a scale, from the domestics who loved me so, from my devout and devoted parents—how could I, now that I've become the stolen goods, the surrendered slave, of an inauspicious abduction—how could I, shut up like a slave in a stockade of stone, shorn and stripped of all the creature comforts to which I was born and in which I was raised, subject to uncertainty concerning my own salvation, subject to the butchery of torture, in the midst of so many robbers, and robbers like these, in the midst of a community of cutpurses and cutthroats who make my flesh crawl—how could I ever cease from wailing and weeping, how could I go on living at all?"

4.25   After such lamentation, bone-weary from the anguish of her mind, the swelling of her throat, and the utter exhaustion of her body, she let her grief-dimmed eyelids droop into sleep. And she had just closed her eyes and for no long time when, all at once, she was startled from that sleep in the grip of delirium. Far more violently and far more vehemently she begins to assault and assail herself, even to beat her breast with furious and open hands and to strike her fine and radiant face. The old woman asks most irresistibly for the reasons behind this new, this renewed grief; nevertheless, with a sigh drawn up from deep down within, thus spake the maiden:

"Oh, make no mistake about it now! Now beyond a shadow of a doubt my life is over and done! Now I kiss all hope of my salvation goodbye! I must most assuredly get me a weapon: a noose, or a sword, or a suicide leap off a cliff!"

Here's what the old woman, plenty upset, had to say to that. With a frowning, frightening face she ordered the girl to speak: *What in the hell she was bawling about? Why, all at once, was she rubbing raw the wounds of unrestrained lamentation when restored to her wits after the soundness of her short sleep?*

"Oh, of course," she said. "You intend, do you, to cheat my boys of the magnificent profit that comes from your redemption? Oh, no: if you go on like this any further, I shall so work my will that you will be burned alive. All those tears of yours robbers never give two cents for: they dismiss and despise them."

4.26   The girl was frightened by these words; she kissed the old woman's hand. "Please, dear mother!" she said. "That's enough of that! Remember the human ties that bind, and come to my aid, if only a little, in my most grievous and pitiless misfortune. For I do not believe that sympathy has absolutely dried up along with these holy grey hairs of yours; no, not in you, who have ripened through all your long years. In short, cast your eyes upon the tragic theater of my trials and tribulations.

"There was a young man, handsome to behold, the leading light among his friends and equals. The whole town chose him as First Citizen, and more than that: he was my cousin, and older than I in age by a mere three years. From our earliest years he was brought up in my company and so grew up, inseparable from me in our living arrangements, in our little house; no, in the same room, in the same bed, bound to me, as I was to him, in the mutual affection of a holy love. Through legitimate nuptial vows he had from long ago been pledged to the bonds of marriage; he had even been named my husband in the official wedding agreement, with the full consent of our parents. In the close company of a thronging crowd of blood relations and relations by marriage, set to assist in these ceremonies, he was making the ritual offerings of sacrificial animals at all the temples and shrines: the house was decked with boughs of laurel, the house was bright with wedding torches, and through it echoed and reechoed the wedding song.

"And then my mother, born to sorrow, was cradling me in her lap, and was dressing me in my wedding finery, just so; she kissed me, repeatedly, with kisses of affection, honey-sweet; in answer to her nervous prayers, she thought to plant the hope of happy children yet to come. Then came the onslaught: without warning, an invasion of cutthroats and cutpurses—it looked like bloodthirsty war, and the naked edges of their furious swords were flaring. But they raised their hands neither to slaughter nor plunder, but massed themselves into a tight and solid formation and straightaway laid siege to our bedroom. Not a single member of the household fought against them; they none of them stood their ground even the slightest bit; and from the lap of my mother, who was frightened out of her wits, they abducted me, victim that I was, lifeless and blood-drained from this brutalizing terror. After the model of the marriage of Attis, or of Protesilaus, so too was my wedding annulled and broken off.

"But what else should I see but that my misfortune is even now renewed—no, new woe is piled on old—in this appalling and brutalizing nightmare of mine. You see, in my dream I had been dragged out of my house, out of my bridal chambers, out of my room, last but hardly least, out of my very bed, and through pathless wastelands went calling out behind me the name of my most woeful and unfortunate husband. And he—the perfume still

4.27

running down his face, his head still crowned in garlands of flowers—as soon as he was widowed from my loving embrace, he was following after me, in my tracks, as I ran away on feet that were not my own. And he whipped up a hue and a cry and lamented the abduction of his beautiful wife and appealed to the people to come to his aid; but one of the robbers, moved to anger by his resentment at this troublesome pursuit, snatched up a big rock that lay at his feet, struck the poor young man that was my husband, and killed him. And I was more than terrified by the dark dreadfulness of a vision like this; in fear and trembling, I was startled awake from a sleep of death."

The old woman drew a deep sigh to hear such tears; then she began as follows:

"Don't panic, my mistress; calm down. There's no need to be terrified by the insignificant figments and fabrications of dreams. To say nothing of the fact that the apparitions of one's daytime repose are shown to be mere lies, it is even the case that the visions and phantasms that come in the nighttime often portend the events that they seem to contradict. Here's the proof: to be in tears, to be beaten, sometimes even to have your throat slit—these portend favorable outcomes, full of profit and prosperity. On the other hand, to laugh, to stuff your stomach full of honey-sweet treats, to come together in the passion of Venus—these foretell that one is to be tormented by sorrow in the soul, sickness in the body, by many another curse as well. But I will talk you out of this straightaway, in elegant storytelling, in the fictions of an old woman."

And so she began:

The Tale Begins

4.28   "Once upon a time there were, in a certain city, a king and a queen, and they had daughters, three in number, astonishing in loveliness. Though the two eldest by birth were exceptionally appealing in appearance, it was thought that their glories could be appropriately sung in human songs of praise. But as for the youngest—her beauty was so exceptional, so outstandingly radiant, that in the poverty of human speech it could not have its measure taken, could not even be approximately praised. In short, herds of her fellow citizens, flocks of foreign visitors, congregated together in eager and curious crowds because of the rumor of such a prodigious spectacle; they stood in attitudes of drop-jawed shock and awe at her unapproachable physical perfection. They would put their right hands to their mouths, would lay the index finger atop an upright thumb, and would in silence worship her in no uncertain terms, in their devotions and venerations, as very Venus, the goddess herself.

"By this time, the story had spread throughout the neighboring cities and the bordering regions that the goddess—she who was born from the depths of the sky-blue sea, she who was nurtured by the salt-spray of the foaming waves—had now deigned to bestow far and wide the grace and favor of her godhead and her power, and was now dwelling in the midst of the throngs of her people; or, if not that, then the earth and not the sea had put forth a new shoot from some miraculous seed, watered by the dews of heaven, a Venus with every flower of maidenhood endowed. And in this way her reputation grows, day by day and astronomically; in this way the story diffuses in different directions, having spread itself now through the neighboring islands, then through more of the mainland, and finally through a fair portion of the provinces. Now many from the wide world round, by long overland journeys, by deepwater travels over the sea, would come together in waves to gaze at this most praiseworthy paradigm of the age. And Venus' island of Paphos? There was no one who would set sail to view the goddess *there,* no one for Cnidos, no one even for Cythera itself. Now Venus' rites and rituals are relinquished, her temples are transformed in squalor, the cushions at her temple-feasts are trampled underfoot, the worship and reverence due her are disregarded: her statues stand ungarlanded, her widowed altars stand foul and filthy under layers of cold ash.

4.29

"But the girl—prayers and offerings are made to *her,* and the powers of the godhead of such a powerful goddess are appeased in the features of a human face. When the maiden would take her morning walk they would offer oblation to the name of Venus in sacrifices both blooded and bloodless—but Venus was not there; when the maiden mixed with them in the streets and marketplaces, the people would mob her and beseech her with flowers bound in garlands, with handfuls of loose flowers. This shameless shifting of heavenly honors to the cult of a mortal maiden sets the anger of the true Venus on fire, and with a vengeance. She could not contain her righteous indignation: she shook her head from side to side; she drew up a groan from deep down within, and this is how she makes her case to herself:

4.30　　　"'So much for me, the ancient and antediluvian mother of the nature of the universe! So much for me, the source that first set the four elements in motion! So much for me, Venus, I who feed and foster the whole of this great globe! I must conduct myself with a mortal girl in some associate status, my divine dignity divided; and my name, set among the stars of heaven, is desecrated, dragged through the dirt of the earth! Oh, of course! It's through rights of expiation directed toward this *name* we have in common that I will be able to endure the ambiguity of veneration through substitution! And shall a girl who's doomed to die carry my image before her as she walks in solemn procession? So it was in vain that the shepherd Paris preferred me to those two great goddesses because of the prodigious paradigm of *my* beauty— Paris, whose justice and faithfulness the great god Jupiter himself endorsed? But she won't be glad, not much, that she, whoever she is, has claimed the honors that are due me by my right, for soon I shall so work my will that she will regret this beauty of hers, beauty to which she has no claim.'

"And so she summons her son to her presence posthaste, the boy with the wings, that reckless, impetuous boy. Through his misbehavior and malfeasance, thumbing his nose at civilization, law, and order, armed with torches and arrows, running at night here and there through homes that are not his own, corrupting marriages through indiscriminate seductions, authoring outrages on an enormous scale—and getting away with it—he is up to absolutely no good. He does as he pleases—that's his inborn nature— and so he's impudent and importunate enough, but she goads him on still further by her words: she takes him to the city and shows him Psyche—for this is the name that the girl went by—face to face.

4.31　　　She puts in evidence the entire fiction about a rival, a rivalry, in beauty; she moans and groans in righteous anger:

"'Now I come to you,' she said. 'I beg you by the bonds of a mother's love, by the luscious lacerations of this your arrow, by the honey-sweet searings of this your torch, avenge the goddess who bore you, avenge her in full. Exact a harsh punishment for this girl's brazen, overbearing beauty, and do this thing, this one thing, for me, and willingly, a solitary thing to wipe the slate clean: let the maiden be held tight in the grip of a torrid, white-hot love for some man who is the lowest of the low, the sort of man whom Fortune has so damned in social status, fiscal wealth, and physical integrity, one so debased and degraded, that in the whole of this great globe he cannot find a match for his misery.'

"Thus spake Venus. She pressed her long and lingering kisses on her son in open-mouthed osculation, then leaves for the nearest shore of the sea, where the waves wash back and forth. As soon as the rosy soles of her feet step on the spray of the summit of the surging of the waves, behold! The depths of the sea settle themselves smooth, the surface dry and bright. And the very wish that she had just begun to wish an orchestration of oceanic obedience hastens to perform, and right instantly too, as if she had earlier given the order. The daughters of Nereus are there, singing a choral song; so too Portunus, with his abundant, bristling, blue-green beard; Salacia, heavy with fish in the folds of her robe; little Palaemon, the charioteer on his dolphin. Now on every side there are companies of Tritons cutting capers on the seas: one makes for her a gentle trumpet blast upon his resounding conch shell; another with awnings of silk shields her from the enemy, the heat of the scorching sun; another holds the mirror before the face of his mistress; still others, yoked two-by-two, swim under and buoy up her chariot. Such is the army of Venus, and such is her escort as she journeys toward the realms of Ocean.

The Bride of Death

"In the meantime, Psyche and that beauty of hers, everywhere acknowledged and admired, enjoys not one benefit from her loveliness and comeliness. All would gaze and all would praise, but not one single man—neither king, nor king's son, nor even the common man—comes forward as a suitor or seeks her hand in marriage. To be sure, they are astounded at the divine paradigm; but all are astounded as if at an image, a statue polished to perfection by some true artist's skill. Her two older sisters long ago had kings for suitors, had been betrothed, and had already

4.32

achieved marriage and wedded bliss, even though the people had spread no news abroad about their modest beauty; but Psyche, now maiden and widow, sitting at home alone, wails and weeps her isolation, her desolation, sick in her body and in agony in her mind; and inwardly, although it captured the imaginations of all the people, she hates that beauty of hers.

"And so that most pitiable father of that most woeful and miserable daughter turns his eyes upward to the angers of heaven and, fearful of the wrath of the gods above, makes inquiry of the most immemorial oracle of Apollo at Miletus, and seeks from his magnificent godhead, through prayers offered and victims slain, a wedding and a husband for the shunned and slighted maiden.—*And Apollo, Greek god and true Ionian though he may be, gave his response in the Latin tongue, in deference to the author of a Milesian tale:*—

4.33   "'High on a crag in the mountains, O king, you must offer your daughter;
      Dress her in ritual robes fit for a wedding with Death.
You may not hope for a son-in-law sprung from a bloodline of humans—
      Only a fell, snake-like beast, wild, sadistic, and cruel.
   Over the heavens it flies on its wings and assails the whole world
      Sapping the strength of each thing, fighting with fire and sword.
Jupiter, feared by the rest of the gods, stands quaking to see it;
      Ghosts on the shores of the Styx tremble before it in awe.'

"The king had once been a blessèd man, but now, after the receipt of the pronouncement of this holy, this awful prophecy, he goes back home again discouraged and despondent, sluggish and slow, and unravels this perplexity, this cursèd response, to his wife. There is sorrow and lamentation, there is wailing and weeping, all the rituals of mourning, for days and days and days. But now the time for the abominable accomplishment of this dreadful response is hard upon them. Arrangements are made for the funeral procession for this most pitiable maiden's wedding with Death. Now the flames in the torches sputter and gutter under ash and black soot; the tune the pipes would play to celebrate the marriage yoke is rekeyed to the fitful, fretful Lydian mode; the wedding song *Hymen, O Hymenaeë* ends in keening and ululation; the girl who is about to be a bride wipes her tears away herself with the corner of her bridal veil. And so it was that the whole city shared in the sorrow of this crippled house and its deplorable doom, and there was proclaimed posthaste a suspension of all public business, in keeping with the universal sorrow.

"All the same, obedience to the warnings of heaven was inevitable, and it drove our sorry little Psyche to the punishment that had been assigned to her. And so, after all the solemn ceremonies for this wedding with Death had been recited and enacted with the greatest of grieving, the entire population of the city follows along as the living corpse is escorted out, and they accompany the sobbing Psyche not to her bridal bed but to her burial. Her mother and her father, in sorrow and in mourning, are driven by the depth of their disaster to hesitate to enact the rest of this unspeakable outrage, but their very own daughter urges them on to it with questions like these:

4.34

"'Why force upon your unfortunate old age the crucifixion of lamentation without cessation? Why assail your spirit, which is more properly my spirit, with wailing unending? All your tears can do no good—why let them corrupt the faces that must compel my devotion and obeisance? Why claw at my eyes by clawing at your own? Why tear your grey hair? Father, why beat your chest? Mother, why beat the breasts that are so holy to me? These, then, are the radiant rewards you reaped of my extraordinary beauty. Too late do you realize that you have been struck the fatal stroke of Envy, unspeakable Envy. When foreign nations and native populations were singing our praises and according us honors that belong to the gods, when in a clear and unanimous voice they named me the new Venus, *then* you should have been in anguish, *then* you should have wailed and wept, *then* you should have mourned for me as for one already dead and gone. Only now do I realize, only now do I see, that my death is caused solely by Venus' name. Lead me on, let me stand upon the crag that the oracle has destined for me. Now I hurry on to keep my date with this happy marriage, now I hurry on to see this nobly born husband of mine. There is no reason for me to delay or decline the arrival of one who was born to destroy the whole of this great globe.'

"So spake the maiden, then held her tongue. Now with a confident and conquering forward stride she made herself a part of the procession that walked along at her side. They arrive at the appointed crag upon the precipitous cliff and there, at the loftiest

4.35

point of its summit, they all abandon her, the sacrificial victim. There too they leave behind the wedding torches that had lighted their way, but only after they had extinguished them with their tears. They hang their heads and make arrangements for the homeward recessional. Psyche's pitiable parents, despondent and despairing after such a dreadful disaster, hid themselves from view in the shadowy recesses of the palace and surrendered themselves to everlasting night. But Psyche, in fear and trembling, apprehensive and unstrung, stands in travail there on the crown of the crag, and the delicate breath of Zephyr, the West Wind, blows gently and ruffles the skirts of her gown all around, and inflates its folds and by soft degrees raises her high into the air; with its gracious inspirations it carries her by soft degrees, gradually and deliberately, down the steep rock face of the towering mountain, then lets her land and lays her lightly in the floral lap of the grassy ground in the valley that lies far below.

The Master of the Golden Palace

5.1   "Psyche lay back at her sweet leisure there in the cushioned, meadowed swale, upon the dew-damp grass, her bed; and now that the discomposition and derangement of her mind had been put to rest, she fell into a sweet slumber. Soon after, recovered and revived by sufficient sleep, she arises with a tranquil spirit and a calm disposition. She sees a grove, planted with enormous and overtowering trees; she sees a spring, bright as day, with water clear as glass; and in the heart of the grove, its focal point, where the spring spills over, there is a palace, a house not made with human hands but a god was its craftsman. When you first set foot across its threshold you would have no doubt that this is the radiant residence of some god, his enchanting Xanadu. Columns of gold, you see, rise to meet the coffered recesses of the high ceiling, carefully carved and chiseled from citron-wood and ivory; all the walls are covered in chased silver reliefs—wild animals, domesticated animals, all sorts, coming to greet their visitors head-to-head. Absolutely miraculous was the man—no, the demigod or, if not that, the god in full—who in the subtle skills of superior art transformed such a mass of civilized silver into wildlife.

"And more than that! Even the tilings of the floor, made of precious stones cut fine, are divided into registers, mosaics in pictures and patterns of all sorts. Tremendously blessèd—yes, and two times and more times over—are they whose feet pass over such gems and strings of jewels! And the other wings of this palace, arrayed from side to side and round about, are similarly precious and priceless, and all of it, with the walls constructed of bricks of gold, flares in a radiant glory all its own, so that the house makes its own day and daylight, even when the sun refuses to shine; so too do all bedrooms, the colonnades, and even the doors explode with their own light. The household goods are no different: in their opulence they match the dignity and grandeur of the palace, so that you would rightly conclude that here is a heavenly imperial residence fashioned by great Jupiter himself so that he may dwell among mortals.

"The place itself delights Psyche and entices her; she comes closer and then, slightly more self-confident, takes herself across the threshold. Her eager enthusiasm for the investigation of this fair, fantastic phantasm draws her further in, and she squints and peers at every detail, and on the far side of the house she catches sight of store-chambers exquisitely crafted in the most surpassing workmanship, chock-full of Titanic treasures. There is nothing that exists that is not there. But, beyond every other cause for her astonishment at opulent objects on such a magnificent scale, this is far and away the most astounding: this treasure house of the whole of this great globe is protected by not a single chain, bolt, or guard. And as she inspects all this with the greatest of passion and delight, a voice presents itself to her, a disembodied voice. 5.2

"'Why, my lady,' it said, 'does your jaw drop at the sight of such a welter of wealth? All these things belong to you. So go to your bedchamber. You are utterly exhausted: revivify yourself in your bed. Go to your bath when you think best. We are your handmaidens, we whose voices you catch on the air, and we will wait on you hand and foot, before you even give the order; and a dinner fit for a queen will not be slow in coming after you have attended to the needs of your body.'

"Psyche realized that her blessèd state was the gift of the gods, of Providence, and so, following the advice and instructions of that invisible voice, she washes away her weariness both by sleep, first of all, and by a bath, soon thereafter. And instantly there appears before her a semi-circular seat, a Greek *sigma*; 5.3

Psyche, deducing from the dinnerware and the appointments of the dining room that this was designed for her refreshment and refection, gladly sits at her ease in it. Right then and there, piled-high platters are set out before her, served by no servant but simply propelled by some breath of air: wines like nectar to drink, foods of every kind to eat. And for all that she could see not a soul, but heard only words as they poured out; voices were the only handmaidens that she had. After her sumptuous supper a man entered and sang, invisible; another plucked the strings of a lyre that similarly could not be seen. Then there was the sound of a singing multitude, one and in harmony, that came to her ears; though there was not a single person to be seen, it was all the same obvious that here was a chorus.

5.4   "But then these passions and pleasures come to an end; the nighttime nudges her, and Psyche goes off to bed. And now it is the depths of night, and a mild and merciful sound reaches her ears. Then, so alone and so unguarded, Psyche is afraid for her virginity; in fear and trembling, she lies quaking, and more than for any evil she is in mortal terror of the unknown. And then the unknown husband is there: he had climbed into the bed, he had made Psyche his wife, and before the sun had risen he had hastily gone away. And instantly the waiting voices that had been stationed in her room attend to the new bride for the virgin life just taken. And over time, all this long time, these actions are repeated, in just this way. To be sure, this is how nature engineers such things: what was new and unanticipated had bestowed joy upon her through accustomed habit and repetition; and the sound of that indeterminate voice was a consolation in her isolation.

Psyche and Her Sisters

"In the meantime, Psyche's mother and father were growing old and worn through their unrelieved grief and mourning. The story spread beyond their kingdom, and the older sisters found out about everything; they left their own homes and, each striving to outdo the other, set out, in sorrow and mourning and tears, to be in the presence of, to have an audience with, their mother and father.

"And on that very night thus spake the husband to his Psyche   *5.5*
(true: there was no part of him that could not be apprehended by
her senses, by hands and ears if not by eyes):

"'Psyche, my wife, my dear, my sweet, sweet Psyche, Fortune
is more sadistic yet. She threatens you with a danger that will
encompass your destruction; it is my considered opinion that
you must be on your guard against it, with due and deliberate
caution. Your sisters are upset by the rumor of your death, and
are following now in your tracks; they will straightaway be at
your crag. Whatever may be the wailings and weepings that you
catch on the air, make no response—no, don't even look in their
direction at all. If you do, you will bring to life the most appalling anguish for me, but for you the very depths of death
and destruction.'

"She nodded *Yes*, and promised that she would do as her husband saw fit; he slipped away even as the nighttime did. But then
the sorry little Psyche wasted the whole day long in tears, beating
her breast, saying again and again that now her life was absolutely over, beyond the shadow of a doubt: she was shut up in
a prison under some blessèd house arrest, widowed, kept from
the company and conversation of her fellow human beings; she
could not even bring to her sisters the solace that would be their
salvation in their sorrow for her; she could not even see them at
all. She did not recover, she did not revive herself, not by bathing,
not by eating—in short, not by any sort of refreshment—but, crying floods of tears, Psyche went away to sleep. There was no   *5.6*
delay. Her husband, arriving somewhat sooner than he should
have, lay at his ease and embraced his Psyche, still crying. He
takes her to task:

"'Are these the promises that you made to me, my Psyche? I am
your husband: what can I expect from you now, what can I hope
for? All day long and all night long and even in wedded embrace
you don't quit your crucifixion. All right then, do as you please.
Be a slave then to your heart's desire, even if it calls for such
prodigal loss. My warning is not to be trifled with, and you will
remember it when, too late in the day, you begin to repent.'

"Then she wrings it out of her husband, by her prayers, by
threatening that her own death is imminent, and he nods *Yes* to
her desires, to let her see her sisters, to mitigate their mourning,
to meet them face to face. And so did he grant his indulgence to
the appeal of his new bride, and more than that: he gave her his

permission to make them gifts of whatever she liked, gold or jewels. But again and again he gave her this warning and frightened her frequently: *She was not to be prevailed upon by her sisters and their catastrophic counsels to find out the physical form of her husband; she was not to go sticking her nose in like some temple robber and so cast herself down into the abyss from the high throne of Fortune's grace; she would never thereafter regain her husband and his embrace.*

"Psyche thanked her husband, and felt more joyful in her heart's desire.

"'I would die a hundred deaths,' she said, 'before I would deprive myself of this sweet, sweet marriage to you. For I love you, whoever you are, and I am out of my mind in longing for you as for my own life's breath; I wouldn't even pit Cupid against you. Yet be generous and grant to me and to my prayers, I pray you, this one more thing; give the order to your servant, the West Wind, to set my sisters here before me, conveyed as I was once conveyed.'

"She presses upon him her kisses of cajolery, she heaps upon him her phrases of coquetry, she wraps around him her soft limbs of urgency, then to her charms and allurements she adds these epithets: *my honey-sweet, my husband dear, O sweet soul of your Psyche.* Against his will, the husband fell beneath her spell, through the power and compulsion of such billing and cooing, like Venus' dove; he promised that he would satisfy her every request; then, as dawn was on the doorstep, he slipped out of the arms of his wife and was gone.

5.7   "Now her sisters had inquired about the crag and had determined the spot where Psyche had been abandoned; impulsively they arrived there, and began to weep their eyes out, to beat their breasts and wail until the rocks and slopes and spurs of the mountain echoed back a sound to match their unending wailing. They tried to summon their luckless sister, calling her by her name, the sound of their wailing voices carrying far and wide, tumbling down the down-sloping mountain, until Psyche ran out of her house like a madwoman, frightened out of her wits.

"'Why do you so assault yourselves,' she said, 'with these wailings and weepings, and all to no purpose? The sister you mourn for—here I am! So, enough of the voices of mourning; and those cheeks of yours, dripping with tears all this time—you may dry them now at last, for now you may take to your arms the sister that you would beat your breasts for.'

"Then she calls the West Wind to her side, and passes on to him the order her husband had given her. There is no delay. Instantly and in obedience to her command he carries them on the most merciful blasts of his breath and conveys them down without injury or incident. Then each to each they take delight in reciprocal embraces and urgent kisses; the tears that had long lain dormant are rightfully returned to them; it is their joy that draws them out.

"'But now it is time,' she said, 'for you to enter under our roof, into our hearth and home, in gladness of heart; in the company of your Psyche your tormented souls may now recover and revive.'

"So she approached and addressed them. Then she reveals to   5.8
them, both to their eyes and to their ears, the inexhaustible wealth of her golden house and the numberless domestic staff of her servant voices; she restores them and refreshes them in lavish extravagance, in a bath of surpassing beauty, in the sumptuous spread at her supernatural table. The result? Gorged and glutted on the gifts that spilled from this—in no uncertain terms—cornucopia of heavenly delights, they now nursed Envy deep in their hearts and close at their breasts. In short, one of the sisters won't stop asking question after question, thoroughly, insightfully, painstakingly: *Who is the lord of all these heavenly manifestations? Who—or what—is Psyche's husband?* Yet for all that, Psyche in no way dishonors the command that came from her husband or lets it be dislodged from the secret recesses of her heart, but she extemporizes and makes up a story: he is a young man, a handsome young man, the soft down only just now darkening his cheeks; his days are chiefly spent in hunting, round about the countryside, up and down the mountains. Still, she doesn't want her silent resolution betrayed by a slip of the tongue in continued conversation, so she fills their arms with wrought gold and jeweled necklaces, instantly calls the West Wind to her side, and entrusts them to his care, to be brought back from where they came.

"And the deed was directly done. Then these extraordinary sis-   5.9
ters, burning with the black bile of an ever-increasing Envy, had much to trumpet back and forth in reciprocal remarks as they made their way back home. Here's the proof; thus spake the first:

"'Would you look at that! Fortune, you *are* blind, and sadistic, and simply unfair! So you were satisfied with this, were you, that we sisters, all born of the same mother and the same father, should shoulder the burdens of such unlike lot and luck? And we two, the older sisters, surrendered to foreign husbands as handmaidens, not wives, outcasts from hearth and home and the country of our birth, are we to live out our lives far, far from our parents as exiles? And this one, the youngest, the terminal kid thrown by her dam's failing fertility—is she to get wealth on such a scale, and a god as a husband? She, who doesn't even know the right and proper use of such lucre, such a treasure trove? Sister, you saw the quality and the quantity of the jewelry that lies in her house, the sheen of the cloth and the clothing, the gorgeous gleam of the gemstones, the mass of the gold that is everywhere trod underfoot besides. And if the husband that she holds in her arms is as beautiful as she's claiming, then there's not a woman alive now in the whole of this great globe who is happier than she is. But beyond all that, as they become more and more accustomed to each other and their mutual affections are reinforced, perhaps this god will make her a goddess as well. Yes, by Hercules, that's it! *That* accounts for how she postured and posed! Now, even now, she has her eyes on heaven; she may be a woman, but she exudes divinity, having voices as handmaidens, laying down the law for the Winds themselves. But *I*—fool that I am—my portion is a husband who is, first of all, even older than my father; he's balder than a bottle-gourd to boot, scrawnier than any child, and he keeps the whole house under lock and key, with door-bolts, bars, and chains.'

5.10   "The second sister takes up where the first left off:

"'Well, *my* husband is tied up in knots with arthritis; he's so bent over with it that I have to settle for pathetically infrequent worshipful attendance at *my* altar of Venus; time and again I have to massage his fingers—twisted, hard as stone—blistering my own dainty and delicate hands with his putrid plasters and disgusting dressings and foul fomentations, settling for the painful and oppressive impersonation of a nurse, not the characteristic countenance of the conscientious wife. Now you, my sister—you can consider carefully just how like a saint, or how like a slave— yes, because I will say what I mean as a free woman should—you mean to put up with all this; but I—no, I can no longer settle for so blessèd a fortune to have befallen one so unworthy of it. I mean, just remember how haughtily, how high-handedly she dealt with us, how she gave away her pride-swollen heart in the very flaunting of that vulgar and distasteful display; how unwillingly she flung at our feet some paltry portion of her overwhelming wealth and then, posthaste, burdened and bored by our being there before her, how she gave the order for us to be whisked, whistled, and wafted away. I am no woman, and I have no breath of life in me at all, if I cannot throw her down to the depths from the pinnacle of her prosperity. And if the insult that she has done to us has left a bad taste in your mouth too, and it's only right that it should, then come, let's find some plan to overpower her, the two of us together. First, let's not reveal to mother and father, or to anyone else, what we are carrying or, even more than that, that we know anything at all about her survival and salvation. It is enough that we have seen what we regretted we saw, without bearing such blessèd tidings to our parents and to all people everywhere. After all, how blessèd can she or anyone be if no one knows of their riches? We are older and she will learn that she has not handmaidens but *sisters.* But for now, let's withdraw and go back to our husbands, return to our poor but proper hearths and homes and then, when the time is right, armed with yet more due and deliberate stratagems and devices, let's come back more highly resolved to punish her pride.'

"This wicked plan satisfies these wicked women as if it were wonderful. They hide away all their oh-so-precious gifts, they tear their hair, they scratch furrows in their cheeks—exactly what they deserved!—and begin their wailing and weeping anew. And in this way, hurriedly and in no uncertain terms, they rub raw each of their parents' griefs and scare them away from learning the truth; then, bloated with bile and madness, they go away to their homes, hatching their hateful, horrible—no, homicidal— plot against their sister, who had done them no wrong.

5.11

Psyche's Pregnancy

"In the meantime, the husband whom she does not know is warning Psyche yet again in those midnight tête-à-têtes of theirs:

"'Surely you see how great a danger hangs over your head? Now Fortune's forces are in the field, fighting from afar, and if you do not take precautions, stern and resolute, soon she will engage you in close-quarter combat. Those hypocritical whores of sisters of yours are laying an abominable ambush against you, exhausting themselves in the effort, and this is their goal in a nut-

shell: to persuade you to search out my face and my features—
and as I've told you time and again before, if you ever see them
once you will never see them again. And so, as for the future, if
those wickedest of witches ever come—and come they will, I
know it—armed with their envenomed anger, you are not even to
speak to them, not a single word. But if you just can't stand to do
that, because of the simplicity of soul that you were born with, because of the tenderness of your heart, then you must at least not
listen to a single question about your husband or offer a single answer. You see, we two shall soon increase our family; this belly of
yours, a child's till now, carries another child, ours, within it: divine, if you protect our secrets in silence; mortal, if you reveal
them to the world.'

5.12   "And at the news Psyche was happy and burst into blossom; for
joy at the consolation portended by this divine child she clapped
her hands; she was impatient for the glory of this future promise;
she was in raptures at the honor and dignity of the name of
mother. Nervously she counts the days as their number swells,
the months as they come and go; from the unfamiliarity of the
bale and burden she bears she is astounded that so great an
incremental growth in the richness of her womb can come from
so transitory a pricking.

"But those unspeakable scourges, those foul Furies, were already hastening on their way, the venom of vipers in their panting breath, sailing over the sea in godless haste. And then, one
more time, here is how her ephemeral husband warns her:

"'Look, Psyche! The last day is at hand, the dawn of the ultimate disaster! Your own sex is sworn against you; your own
blood is your enemy; they have shouldered their arms, broken
their camp, drawn up their battle lines and sounded the call to
battle; with their swords unsheathed your sacrilegious sisters
seek to slit your throat. Curses! O my sweet, sweet Psyche, what
catastrophes and cataclysms close in around us! *Misericordia!*
Have pity on yourself; have pity on us; scrupulously safeguard
our secrets; from the woe and misery of the utter destruction that
is on the horizon let your household go: your husband, yourself,
and this our little child. And those daughters of doom—you must
not call them sisters, not after their hatred that would hound you
to your death, not after they have trampled underfoot the bonds
and obligations of blood—you must not look at them, you must
not listen to them. When they are perched on that crag like the

Sirens, their voices will make the rocky cliff-face ring, voices that will bring death and destruction.'

"Psyche took up where he left off, but stifled her speech with tears and convulsive sobbing:

"'You have often before now, so far as I can tell, weighed in the balance the proofs of my obedience and of my reticence. This time will be no different, and now the inflexibility of my mind shall prove itself acceptable to you yet again. You just give the order again to our good servant the West Wind, have him fulfill your will, as is his obligation; then give me at least the sight of my sisters if not the epiphany of your sacred shape that you have denied to me. Please, then, by these your curls with their scent of cinnamon, hanging here, and here, and here; by these your cheeks, so soft, so smooth, so like my own; by this your breast that burns with a heat I cannot fathom; by this your face that I hope at least to come to know in this our little child: I am beside myself; I am your suppliant; I invoke you by these my pious prayers—humor me, grant me the enjoyment of my sisters' embraces, and let the soul of your Psyche, so devoted and dedicated to you, recover and revive in joy. And as to this face of yours, I make no more demands; nothing stands in my way now, not even these shadows, this nighttime; you are my light, and I hold you in my arms.'

"With these incantations whispered over him, these words, these pliant embraces, her husband wiped away her every tear with his hair; he promised that he would do as she asked, and instantly left before the light of the new day arrived.

"Psyche's double yoke of sisters, a conspiracy sworn and bound, do not even stop to see their parents; straight from the ships they make for that crag at a whirlwind pace; they do not even wait for the appearance of that fair, transporting wind but with a self-satisfied recklessness they leap out into the abyss of the air. The West Wind, though unwilling, was not unmindful of the royal decree; he enfolded them in the bosom of his soft-blowing breezes and settled them on solid ground. But they do not dawdle; instantly and in lockstep they invade the interior of the house; giving the lie to the name they embrace Psyche not as sister but as spoils, and beneath their smiling faces they bury deep down their own treasure house of deceit and deception. And this is how they fawn and flatter:

"'Psyche! You're no longer the little girl you were before, but are now a mother yourself! Do you have any idea how great a gain for us all you carry in this little belly of yours? O how happy you shall make our whole household! What great delights shall be ours! How blessèd will we sisters be when nursing and raising this golden, holy child! And if his beauty is a match for the beauty of his parents—as would only be right—he shall in no uncertain terms be born a Cupid.'

5.15   "And this was the way they lay siege to the soul of their sister, gradually and deliberately, with pretense of affection. They were utterly exhausted from their trek, and instantly, after she re-vivifies them with a comfortable seat and attends to their bodies with soothing baths of vaporous heat, Psyche entertains them lavishly in her dining room with her marvelous, her blessèd, foods and pâtés and savory meat. She gives the order for the lyre to speak, and there is playing; for the pipes to perform, and their sound is heard; for the chorus to sing, and there is music. All of these together soothed the spirits of those who heard them with their sweet, sweet strains, though there was not a one of them to be seen.

"But for all that, the wickedness of these women of doom was not to be softened even by such honeyed sweetness of song, was not lulled to sleep. No, but to the predetermined shackles and snares of their own deceits and deceptions they bent and twisted the conversation. Disguising their desires they initiated their interrogation: *What sort of a husband did she have? Where was he born? What did he do for a living?* And then? Well, she forgets the conversation they'd had earlier and, too guileless, too simpleminded, she fashions a brand-new falsehood. She says that her husband comes from the next province over, is a big businessman turning big profits, is now well into his middle age, the hairs on his head flecked with white. And on this new conversation she spent not more than a moment of her time; once again she filled her sisters' arms with gifts of lavish extravagance and returned them to their

5.16   conveyance of thin air. They were raised on high by the West Wind's serene spirit but then, as they make their way back home, this is how they talk back and forth between themselves:

"'Really, sister, what can we say about that little fathead's bald-faced and monstrous lie? First it was a handsome young man, just now decked out in a beard of blossoming down; now it's a man in his middle age, his head bright with the light of white hair. Who is this man who has undergone such a metamorphosis in such a short space of time to such a sudden old age? You will find,

O sister mine, no other explanation but this: either that worst of women is lying and making all this up, or she has no knowledge of the appearance of her husband. Whichever of these two may be true, we must banish her from her wealth and wherewithal at once. If she does not know her husband's face, then without any doubt she's gone and married a god, and it is a god—god help us—that her pregnancy now brings to term. Make no mistake: if she is going to be known as the mother of a divine child—perish the thought—then I will tie myself a noose and hang myself with it forthwith. But in the meanwhile, let's make our way back home to our mother and father and let's weave onto the warp of this conversation as rosy a web of a ruse as we can.'

The Plot against the Monstrous Husband

"And that is how they set themselves afire. They paid a callous and calculated call on their parents; they lost a night to tossing and turning and wakefulness; in the morning they fly off to that crag. From there they fly down with a vengeance with the accustomed aid and assistance of the wind; they force the tears from their eyes by the rubbing of their eyelids; and this is how they cunningly confront their Psyche:

"'You—well, you're happy enough, blessèd through your ignorance of the magnitude of this evil; you sit there unconcerned about the danger that you're in, while *we*—we stand guard and keep watch over your affairs, sleeping not a wink; your wholesale destruction is our luckless crucifixion. Why? Because this one thing we know to be true and we, being, as you very well know, your companions in your misfortune and your anguish, cannot hide it from you: it is a snake of vast proportions, writhing in countless knots and coils, its jaws running with blood and lethal venom, its mouth gaping open into a bottomless throat, that is lying with you, at your side in the nighttime—and you don't even realize it. Remember now the oracle of Apollo, Python-slayer, trumpeting that you have been foredoomed to a marriage with a deadly monster. Many are the country-folk, many are those who

hunt round about in these parts, who have seen him—and a good
number of those who live nearby as well—returning in the
evening from his feeding and swimming in the shallows and the
5.18   pools of the neighboring stream. And all of them swear that he
will not go on fattening you much longer with his sweet-talking,
subservient care, and feeding. No, but as soon as your full womb
brings your pregnancy to its completion, he'll swallow you down
then, a richer and a plumper dish. In the face of these facts, it's
now up to you to decide whether you want to say *Yes* to your sisters who are so worried about your precious safety, to turn aside
from death and to live with us safe and secure from all alarm, or
whether you want to be buried in the belly of this most sadistic of
beasts. But if the singing solitude of this sylvan spot delights you,
or the foul and danger-fraught fornications of your cloak-and-
dagger desires, or the embraces of your venomous viper—make
no mistake, we your faithful and conscientious sisters shall have
done our duty.'

"Poor little Psyche! So simple of soul, so delicate of heart!
Next thing, she was swept away by her fear of these oh-so-
discouraging words; she found herself beyond the boundaries of
her rational mind; the memory of all her husband's warnings and
all her own promises she let spill completely away, and she
hurled herself headlong into a bottomless pit of trials and tribulations. Her knees were like water; her face was ghastly pale and
bloodless; and these were the words she managed to croak out at
her sisters on her third attempt, her voice escaping from a half-
opened mouth:

5.19   "'You, my dearest sisters, you stand by the obligation of your
love and devotion, as is only right, and those who swear to you
that these tales are true are not just engaging in falsification, or so
it seems to me. Why? Because I have not seen my husband's face,
not once, and I have absolutely no idea where he comes from. I
follow the orders of voices that come to me only at night; I endure
a husband of a nature that I cannot determine, who runs from the
light of every dawn and no exceptions. I really must agree with
you when you say that he is some sort of a monster. Why? Because he always does his utmost to scare me away from any view
of his visage and he threatens that some awful evil will come
from my sticking my nose into questions of his appearance. So
now, if you are able to bring your sister some sort of help to work
her salvation in her jeopardy and her peril, stand firm in your

defense of her now. If you don't, if any *laissez-faire* feeling were to follow, it would render null and void the good work of your earlier Providential precaution.'

"Then it was that these women, this criminal cohort, found the heart of their sister laid bare; the gates had been thrown open and the subterfuges of their secret siege-engines were set aside. With the swords of their skullduggery now unsheathed, they lay siege to the thoughts of the simple soul of the girl, now scared out of her wits. Here's the proof—here is how the one of them began: 5.20

"'The ties of birth that bind us do compel us not to dwell even on dangers that are right before our eyes, not when *your* safety is concerned. Therefore, we will point you down the only road that can lead you to the salvation that we have long time pondered, and long time again. A fine knife, razor-sharp, whetted and honed in the softness of the palm of your hand—take it and hide it in secret in that part of your bed where you usually lie. A lamp, ready for the purpose, full of oil, glowing with a bright light—place it under the cover of some sort of pot for protection, and keep all these preparations and paraphernalia hidden under lock and key. And then, after he comes slithering his rutted way and climbs up into the bed of his routine, and then lies there at length wrapped in the coils and the web of his heavy sleep and starts to snore his stertorous slumber out his nostrils—then you softly slide out of the bed and slowly take your barefoot, mincing, high-arched steps one at a time, release the lamp from the prison of its blinding shadow, take your cue from the counsel of your lamp as to the most opportune moment for your radiant crime, take that two-edged blade and in one bold stroke, your hand raised high aloft, with effort as overmastering as you can exert, cut off from that poisonous serpent the knot of neck and head. You shall not want for our assistance. No, but as soon as you have effected your own salvation by his extermination, we who will be beside ourselves in waiting will fly to you; we will take you and all these riches back with us and will join you, in the marriage we have prayed for, to a human husband as a human bride.'

"The little sister was already aflame, and in no uncertain terms; 5.21 but now her whole being was set to burning, stoked by this inferno of words. They abandon her straightaway, and prodigious is their fear of contact and contagion with such an evil deed. Caught up by the expected blast of the wingèd wind they are laid to rest upon the crag; right then and there they rush off; they

make a swift getaway; instantly they get aboard their waiting
ships and set sail for home. As for Psyche, she is left all alone, except that no one hounded by the furious Furies is ever alone; like
the swells of the sea she rides the crests and troughs of her grief;
although her decision is immovable, although her mind is most
stubbornly resolved, all the same, now that it is time to put her
hand to the crime, she reels like a drunken man, now uncertain of
her decision, pulled in every different direction by the many passions of her trials and tribulations. She hurries, she hesitates; she
is forceful, she is fearful; she is ambivalent, she is angry; and the
acme of her anxiety is that in one and the same body she hates the
monster and loves the husband.

The Revelation

"But for all that, now that evening is bringing nighttime in its
train, in headlong haste she gets ready all her preparations and
paraphernalia for her sacrilegious crime. Then it was night; her
husband had come; first he fought on the fields of Venus; then he
5.22   sank into a deep, deep sleep. Psyche was, as a rule, weak in body
and weak in heart; yet, for all that, with sadistic Fate to supple-
ment her strength, she feels her spine stiffen. She brings out the
lamp, grabs the knife, and in her daring makes herself a man. But
just as soon as the lamp is brought to bear and the secrets of her
bed are illuminated, she sees the mildest of monsters, the sweetest of beasts, CUPID himself, the beautiful god, lying beautifully
asleep. At the sight of the god, the light of the lamp leapt for joy
and blazed brighter, and the knife now felt its first remorse for its
irreverent razor's edge. Not so Psyche: she is immobilized by
such a sight, her heart in another's possession; she is in travail,
the color draining from her ashen face; her knees are like water,
and she sinks down onto her heels. She tries to hide the knife, but
in her own breast; she would have done it too, without any doubt,
if the knife hadn't flown out of her reckless hands in fear of so
outrageous an offense.
    "Now utterly debilitated, forsaken by her salvation—as she
gazes long and longer upon the heavenliness of those features divine, in her mind she is brought back to life. She sees the luxuri-

ous hair of his golden head, intoxicatingly perfumed with ambrosia; his neck, white as milk; his cheeks, ruddy as roses; meandering over them are locks and ringlets, attractively arranged,
some hanging down before, some hanging down behind, and
compared to the superabundant lightning flashes of its radiant
glory the very light of the lamp was only a flicker. Across the
shoulders of the airborne god were feathers gloriously white in
the flashing of their dewy bloom; although his wings were at rest,
the diaphanous and delicate barbs at the edges of his feathers
quivered and rustled and delighted in their restless agitation. The
rest of the body was hairless and smooth, the skin translucent—
Venus would not be ashamed to have given birth to *this*.

Lying before the pedestal of the bed were his bow, his quiver,
and his arrows: a great god's great-hearted weapons. And as   5.23
Psyche subjects these weapons to study—her heart can brook no
restraint, and she has to stick her nose in, in any event—as she
turns them over in her hands and is astounded—she pulls one of
the arrows out of its quiver and tries to test the sharpness of its
point by pricking her thumb. But the force applied by her still
trembling hand was too effective: it pierced her too deep, so that
tiny drops of rose-red blood besprinkled the surface of her skin
like dew. And that was how Psyche, all unknowing, fell in love
with Love of her own free will. And then, more and more in the
grip of a white-hot cupidity for Cupid, forward and insistent, out
of her mind, gazing upon him dumbfounded, she impulsively
smothered him with kisses, open-mouthed and immodest, yet
was afraid: *How deep was he sleeping?*

"Excited by this great goodness but still wounded in her mind,
she rides the crests and troughs; but as she does so, that lamenta-
ble lamp—Was it from some damnable duplicity? Some envenomed Envy? Or was it just impatient just to touch such a body, to
kiss it, as it were, for itself?—spat out from the tip of its spout a
drop of burning oil onto the god's right shoulder. Oh no! Reckless
lamp! Bold as brass! You are Love's lackey, easily bought and sold!
Would you burn the lord and master of all fire everywhere, when
it was some lover, as everyone knows, who first invented you so
he could gain the object of his desire for some longer time, even in
the dead of night? And this is how the god was scalded; he leapt
to his feet; he saw himself contaminated by a confidence that was
now uncovered; he flew away from the kisses and embraces of his
most miserable wife in absolute and unbroken silence.

5.24   "And Psyche instantly and with both her hands grabs his right leg as he rises, a poor and pitiable tailpiece to his atmospheric ascent, his baggage train, his camp-follower floating through the regions of the cloud-studded sky, but at last she falls to earth exhausted. But the god, her lover, did not abandon her as she lay on the ground. He flew to a cypress nearby and here is how he spoke to her from the height of its crown—he was deeply moved:

"'O Psyche! So simple, O so simple of soul! It was I who forgot the commands of my mother Venus. She had given the order for your captivity by your cupidity to some wretched man, the lowest of the low, to be given over to a debased and degraded marriage, but I flew to you as a lover instead. Now I know full well that I did this thing carelessly—yes I, the radiant archer, I struck myself with my own weapon, I made you my wife, just so, I suppose, I could seem to you to be a monster, so you could cut off my head with a sword, because my head held these eyes, the eyes that fell in love with you. Again and again I made my determination known, that you had ever to be on your guard against such things; I warned you and I warned you, out of the kindness of my heart. But your sisters, your incredible consultants and confidantes, they shall pay the price and on the double for such malevolent commandments—*you* I shall punish only by my running away.'

"And at the conclusion of his address he shot up into the abyss of the air on his wings.

Psyche Abandoned

5.25   "Now Psyche lay stretched out upon the ground; she followed into the distance, as far as her vision allowed, the wingèd trajectory of her husband; then she harried her heart in wailings and weepings of the worst sort. He was taken from her *on the oarage of his wings,* as the poets say; and after his extension to the horizon put him in another world, Psyche threw herself headlong from the banks of the nearby brook. But the flowing river, meek and mild, in honor, no doubt, of the god who would burn the very waters as a matter of course, would not put itself at risk but posthaste conveyed her in the gentle coils of its current to a riverbank overgrown with the greenest grass.

"Now it happened that Pan, that god of the countryside, was just then sitting on the brow of the bank of the stream; Echo, that mountain goddess, was in his embrace; he was teaching her to sing in response to the call of every voice and sound. Close by on the riverbank are his goats, cropping the verdure of the river, cutting capers and delighting in their browsing and meandering. In his mercy the shaggy goat god summons Psyche into his presence, wounded as she was and in travail—he was, somehow or other, not unaware of her catastrophe—and this is how he soothes her with his tranquil, calming words:

"'Pretty little girl, yes, I am a man of the countryside and a herder of goats, but thanks to a long-winded and long-winding old age and abundant experience I am quite worldly-wise. If I guess right and guess the truth—and this is without a doubt what the philosophers mean when they say "divination"—then by your staggering steps, like a drunken man's, more often unsteady than not; by your body's acute and ashen pallor; by your perpetual panting and sighing; and more than that, by your pale and languid eyes: you are suffering from love and its excess. Now you listen to me! Never again! Do not destroy yourself in a suicide leap or in any other manner of death that you bid come to you. Abandon this attitude of mourning, set aside your sorrow and your grief, and in your prayers worship Cupid instead, the greatest of the gods; and as he is also a young man, sensitive and sensuous, work to regain his good graces through your tender attentions.'

Psyche's Revenge

"So spoke the goatherd god; Psyche makes no speech in response. She merely makes reverence to the godhead that had worked her salvation and goes on her way. But after she had wandered and trekked a good long way in staggering, travailing steps, all unknowing she comes by some little path at the dying of the day to a city, the city where the husband of one of her sisters had his kingdom. After Psyche realizes this, she longs to have her presence announced to her sister, and is presently brought in to her. Her sister kisses and greets Psyche, Psyche kisses and greets

5.26

her sister, and when their embraces had ended, here is how Psyche begins to answer the question about how it was she came there:

"'You remember the advice that you two gave me: you know, how you persuaded me to kill with a two-edged knife the monster who rested by my side, who lied about the name of husband, to kill it before it swallowed the dear departed down its ravening jaws? The plan pleased me as well, but when I first laid eyes on his face, courtesy of my coconspirator, the light of my lamp, I saw an astounding sight, absolutely divine: it was the very son of the goddess Venus herself, Cupid himself, I say, sleeping there in tranquil repose. I was excited by the sight of this great goodness, confused and upset by this too-great opportunity of passion and delight; but simultaneously, through some miserable mischance, don't you know, a drop of burning oil bubbled over from the lamp down onto his shoulder. He was instantly startled out of his sleep in anguish, and when he saw me with my weapons of fire and sword, he said: "You! Because of this cruel and calamitous crime, divorce yourself from this my bed forthwith! You may keep all your possessions, but I shall join myself in solemn and lawful marriage to your sister!" He gave your given name, then instantly gave the order to the West Wind to blast me away beyond the precincts of his palace.'

5.27   "Psyche hadn't even finished her speech when the sister, whipped on by the twin lashes of tumultuous lust and envenomed rivalry, deceived her husband with a lying story that she extemporized, pretending that she had heard some news about the death of her parents. She instantly gets onboard a ship and goes off straightaway to that crag. Although it was a different breeze that was then blowing, nevertheless, it was in blind hope that she spoke with her mouth gaping open to the wind: *Take me in your arms, O Cupid, a worthy wife; West Wind, lift your mistress up!* Then she threw herself headlong in a monumental leap. But for all that she could not reach her goal, not even as a corpse. Her arms and legs were torn from her body and strewn among the boulders of the rock face; her guts were ripped open, just as she deserved; she died bringing easily accessible edibles to the birds of the air and the monstrous beasts.

"And the punishment that was the subsequent avengement wasn't slow in coming either. You see, Psyche, once again on wandering feet, arrived at another city in which the other sister dwelt under similar circumstances. This sister did no different: she was herself enticed by sisterly deceitfulness; as a competitor for the other sister's wicked wedding she rushed off to the crag and fell to her death and destruction just as the other had.

Venus Learns the Truth

"Now in the meanwhile, as Psyche was making the rounds of the nations, passionate in the pursuit of her Cupid—believe it or not, he himself was lying in his own mother's bedchamber, moaning and groaning, in anguish over the burn from the oil lamp. Just then a bird, the tern, white-on-white, that swims over the waves of the sea on its wings, dives down in haste to the depths of Ocean. And there the tern settles in right next to Venus, just as she was bathing and swimming, and tells her the tale of her scalded son, sorrowing and lamenting over the anguish of his grievous burn, lying in bed, uncertain of his own salvation. And more: in the mouths of all the people of all the nations Venus and her whole family now had a bad reputation, rumor on rumor and slander on slander: 5.28

"'You two have gone into hiding, he by whoring in the mountains, you by swimming in the sea, they say: and that is why there is no passion, no captivation, no attraction, no sophistication, but all is unkempt, unclean, uncultured, and uncouth; there are no marriages between men and women, no camaraderie between friends, no affection among siblings, but only contamination spread far and wide: repulsion, revulsion, tawdry, tasteless copulation.'

"So prattled that wordy bird in Venus' ear, sticking its beak well in, tearing the son's reputation to shreds. And all at once Venus, four-square furious, cries out:

"'Aha! So now that good little son of mine has got himself a girlfriend, has he? You are the only one who serves me out of love—come now, give me her name, the one who tempted and seduced this freeborn, underaged, naked boy, be she one of the nation of the Nymphs, or the number of the Hours, or the chorus of the Muses, or even from the Graces who attend me.'

"That gossiping bird did not keep silent.

"'I do not know, good mistress,' said the tern, 'but I think it is a mortal girl that he's out of his mind in love with, and if I remember right well, she goes by the name of Psyche.'

"Then Venus in righteous indignation cried out, quite loud indeed:

"'He loves *Psyche?* Really? The girl whose beauty pushed mine aside, whose name is in competition with my own? Oh, of course! That little Johnny-come-lately thought I was some bawd, some go-between, that I might point the girl out to him so he could get to know her!'

5.29   "She lost no time. With these protestations on her lips she shot up out of the sea and rushed off straightaway to her golden bedchamber and found her son an invalid, just as she'd been told. And right away, right from the very doorway, she yelled at him as loud as she could.

"'Is this your idea of respectability?" she said. 'Does this befit your birth and mine, your good and honest nature? First, that you should crush my commands beneath your heel—me, not your mother but your master! That you did not submit my mortal enemy to the crucifixion of a foul and bestial love but even clasped her to your bosom in your underdeveloped and oversexed embraces—at your age! Just so I could have my enemy, I suppose, to put up with as a daughter-in-law? Is it conceivable that you suppose that you alone are the breeder, born and bred, and that I because of effete old age can now no longer conceive? You lounging, lazy, unlovely Lothario! All right then, I just want you to know that I will give birth to another son far greater than you; no, I'll adopt one, from among the sons of my slave girls— just to make you feel the cut of my contempt all the more—and I'll give to him those wings of yours, those torches, that bow, those arrows, all my paraphernalia of passion—I had not given them to you for these ends. You know there was nothing that you inherited from your *father's* estate set aside for this sort of getup.

5.30   "'But you were badly warped from the first, from infancy, sharp with your hands and your aim. You struck your elders again and again, showing them no respect; and your very own mother, me my own self, I mean, you strip naked on a daily basis, you assassin; you have struck me often and oftener, evidently despising me as a defenseless widow and having no fear of your stepfather, that mightiest of warriors, the bravest of the brave. And why not? It has been your habit to toast his health with pretty girls, often and oftener, mistresses for the suffocation of my soul. But now I shall so work my will that you will regret this game of yours, that you will realize this marriage of yours is a bitter thing, vinegar in the mouth.

[*Aside*] "'But what can I do, now that I have been held up for ridicule? Who will take me in? With what devices can I keep this cheat in check? Can I beg help from sober-sided Abstinence, my enemy, whom I have insulted, often and oftener, through this boy's indulgence and sensuous extravagance? Absolutely not! I shudder at the thought of a tête-à-tête with that unsophisticated, shabby, sordid woman. Nevertheless, the consolation of vindication must not be despised, wherever it may come from. She is absolutely the one I need at my side, she and no one else, to punish this lazy lounger with extreme prejudice, to strip him of his quiver, to neutralize his arrows, to unstring his bow, to snuff out his torch—no, more than that: to beat his very body into submission with even more bitter remedies. For only then shall I believe that he has paid in full for the insult and injury he has done me, when Abstinence has shaved off the hairs of his head, hairs on which I have with these my hands forever and a day bestowed their gentle, golden glow; when she has clipped off the wings that in my bosom I have bathed from fonts of nectar.'

The Interventions of Ceres and Juno

"Thus spake Venus. She rushes out the door furious, fuming, dyspeptic as only Venus could be. But straightaway Ceres and Juno cross her path. They saw that her face was swollen, and they asked her why she was constricting the alluring charms of her flashing eyes under such a baleful brow.

"'We are well met,' she said. 'The heart within me burns and you are here, don't you know, to effect its will and desire. Use all your strength and all your art, I pray you, and find Psyche for me, that runaway, flyaway girl. For it is inconceivable that the scandalous tale told about my house and the unspeakable deeds of my son have escaped your notice.'

"Now they were not unaware of all that had happened, and here is how they tried to assuage Venus' sadistic anger:

5.31

"'Good mistress Venus, what crime has your son committed that merits all this fuss? That you would do battle against his passions and delights with the relentless anger of your heart? That you would be impatient to destroy the girl he loves as well? Tell us, we pray you, what crime is it for your boy that he gave a willing smile to an elegant girl? Are you unaware that he is male, and young? Or, if not that, then have you forgotten just how old he is now? Or does he always seem to you to be a boy, because he wears his years so prettily? Now you are a mother and, what's more, a woman who knows what's what; are you always going to be poking around and sticking your nose into his dalliances and diversions? Will you find fault with his indulgence and sensuous extravagance, will you convict him for his love affairs, will you censure in your own beautiful son your own devices and desires, your own creature comforts? What god above, what mortal below will put up with this, with you sowing the seeds of love and lust at large throughout the nations, while constricting in your bitterness the loves of your own household, while shuttering that factory of universal access, where female faults are fashioned?'

"And that was how the goddesses, out of fear of his arrows, tried to flatter Cupid, though he was nowhere in sight, playing the part of his prejudiced patrons. But Venus, full of righteous anger that the insults done to her were being taken so lightly, forestalls any further talk and takes to the road in the other direction, with wings on her feet, toward the open ocean.

6.1   "In the meantime, Psyche was tossed this way and that, wandering every which way, all the days and all the nights obsessed with the quest for her husband; and the greater the agony in her soul the greater her cupidity to win him over—certainly with the entreaties of his slave, if she could not calm him with the enticements of his wife, as angry as he was. She caught sight of a temple atop the summit of a steep mountain and said to herself: *Could it be that my good master lives there?* Right then and there she points herself in that direction and quickens her pace: hope and dedication spurred on the steps that labored and staggered after her everlasting efforts. Without hesitation she climbed up over the higher reaches of the rock face, then drew closer to the shrine. She sees stalks of wheat in a heap, stalks of wheat woven into crowns; she sees stalks of barley too. There were sickles and all the apparatus of harvest time, but lying scattered on all sides, carelessly jumbled together, just as they fell from the hands of the farmers, as you'd expect in the Summer's heat. Psyche sticks her nose in and sorts these things out, one by one, removes them into discrete groups and arranges them in right order; she reasons, don't you know, that she ought not slight the shrine or the rite of any god, but should petition the pity and the charity of them all.

"Ceres, bountiful mother, catches her in the act, tending to these things carefully and with cautious concern, and straight-away makes this leisurely complaint: 6.2

"'Are you serious? Poor, pitiable Psyche! Venus, in the frenzy of her soul, is following now in your tracks throughout the whole of this great globe; she is just beside herself; she is after you to sub-ject you to the ultimate punishment; with all her strength, all her divine power, she demands revenge. But *you*—you are taking care of what belongs to me, and thinking about anything else except your own salvation.'

"Then Psyche threw herself down at her feet, watered the god-dess' feet in floods of tears, swept the ground with her hair, and kept on begging her forgiveness, producing polymorphic, poly-phonic prayers:

"'I beseech you, by this your right hand that makes the grain grow; by the rites and rituals of harvest after harvest that guaran-tee their fertility; by the ineffable secrets contained in your baskets at the Thesmophoria; by the wingèd chariots with the snakes that are your attendants; by the furrows and fissures that split the rich soil of Sicily; by Proserpina your daughter—the chariot that stole her, the earth that holds her, the downward path to her pitch-black wedding, the upward path to her bright white revelation—; by everything else that your sanctuary at Eleusis in Attica protects in holy silence: come to the aid of the suppliant soul of your poor, pitiable Psyche. Grant that I may keep myself out of sight here, in among these sheaves of wheat, just a few days and no more, until in the passing of time the sadistic anger of that great goddess may be mollified; or, if not that, then until my own weakness and bone-weariness, brought on by unbroken toil and travail, may be ame-liorated by a momentary intermission and rest.'

"Ceres takes up where Psyche leaves off: 6.3

"'Believe me, I am deeply moved by your tears and prayers, and I really do want to come to your aid, but she is bound to me by ties of blood; more than that, I carefully maintain a time-honored treaty of friendship with her; furthermore, she is a good woman, and I just can't risk incurring any bad feeling. So leave these precincts straightaway; you may take it as a blessing that I have not arrested you and put you under lock and key.'

"Her hopes disappointed, spurned and rejected and now assaulted with a two-fold sorrow, Psyche retraces her downwards path and catches sight of a shrine in a sun-stippled grove of trees in a valley down below her, cunningly and craftily constructed. Unwilling to pass by any path, however improbable, toward her higher hopes, and willing to approach any god or any goddess for grace and favor, she draws closer to the shrine's devoted doorways. She sees offerings and donations of great price, clothing embroidered with letters of gold, all hanging on the branches of trees and the posts of the doors, all commemorating the name of the goddess to whom they had been dedicated out of thankfulness for her interventions. She bends the knee and with her arms embraces the warmth of the altar; first she wipes away her tears, and this is how she then addresses her prayers:

6.4   "'O sister, O wife, of great Jupiter, be thou in Samos, where you keep the age-old sanctuary that alone rejoices in your coming to birth, in the cries of your infancy, in your rearing as a child; or be thou in Carthage of the lofty towers, where you visit the blessèd abode where you are worshipped as a maiden riding up to heaven on the conveyance of a lion; or be thou on the banks of the river Inachus, where you rule over the far-famed walls of the Argives, where you are celebrated as the bride of the Thunderer, as the queen of goddesses; thou whom all the Eastern lands worship as Zygia, Mistress of Marriage; thou whom all the Western lands call Lucina, Goddess of Childbirth—be thou for me now in the extremity of my need Juno Sospita, Lady of Salvation. Behold me, exhausted from the labors that I have drained to the dregs, and free me from my fear of the harm and the hazard that are on the horizon. So far as I can tell, it is your nature to come to the aid of us women who are great with child, when our lives are in peril, even *without* being asked.'

"Such are the supplications of Psyche, and in instant response Juno makes herself manifest to her in all the awful majesty of her divinity. Straightaway she said:

"'O how I wish I could give the nod to your prayers and bend my will to your wishes! But it is shame that will not let me offer assistance in opposition to the will of Venus: she is my daughter-in-law, and I have always loved her as if she were my daughter indeed. And another thing: there are laws that forbid another person's runaway slaves from being taken in without their master's consent—my hands are tied.'

"Psyche was more than terrified: now shipwrecked by Fortune yet again and still unable to overtake her wingèd, flyaway husband, she abandoned all hope of salvation, and here is how she conferred with the thoughts in her own mind: 'What other aid and assistance can now be sought, can now be assayed, in my distress and destitution, when not even the support of goddesses, who are willing enough, can do me any good? Where can I turn my wandering steps when my feet are caught in snares like these? Under whose roof or in what murk and shadow can I hide from and escape the inexorable eyes of great Venus? So why don't you finally wrap a man's courage around you, kiss your vain and threadbare hopes boldly goodbye, surrender yourself to your good mistress even without being asked, and soothe her savage, sadistic impulses by some becoming, though belated, bashfulness? Who knows? You may even find there in the house of his mother the man you have so long been seeking.'

"That was how she was rehearsing the opening words of the petition she was planning, prepared for the uncertainties of submission and subservience; prepared, in fact, for definite destruction.

The Proclamation of Venus

"Now as for Venus—she washes her hands of these remedies, this earthbound hunting-down. She gives orders that her chariot be made ready, the one that Vulcan the goldsmith had polished and perfected for her in painstaking detail, in minute and marvelous manufacture, and had given to her as a wedding gift before his first trial of the wedding bed. The chariot was conspicuous for what had been filed away by the refining rasp, made the more precious by the *loss* of the gold from which it was made. Round about their good mistress's bedchamber are stabled many doves: four of them now come forth, white in color and joyful in step; they rotate their iridescent necks and fit them to their jeweled yoke; with their mistress now in tow they take to the skies rejoicing. Sparrows follow the goddess' chariot, flitting in delight, in wanton flight, chattering and keeping it noisy company, and all

6.5

6.6

the other birds that sing sweet songs make the heavens harmoniously reecho with their honeyed warblings as they announce the coming of the goddess. The clouds make way: Caelus—Heaven himself—opens wide open for his daughter; ethereal Ether, father of Heaven, joyfully receives the goddess with open arms. This euphonious escort of great Venus has no fear of being intercepted by eagles or harried by hawks.

6.7   "Then she points herself straightaway toward the royal palace of Jupiter and with imperious insistence demands to borrow her boisterous brother's backing, the god Mercury: *Indispensable*, she says. Jupiter's dark-blue brow does not nod *No*. Then, right then and there, Venus in triumph descends from her heavenly heights, with Mercury striding alongside her; with careful concern she weaves her wreath of words around him: 'O my brother, child of Arcadia, you surely know that your sister Venus has never done a thing without her Mercury at her side; it must also not have escaped your notice for what a long time now I have been unable to uncover where my handmaiden has squirreled herself away. So there's nothing else to do about it: publication and promulgation must be made by your proclamation, that there is ample compensation for revealing her location. Therefore, bring my command to its swift completion; catalogue in clear detail the characteristics by which she may be identified—I don't want anyone to plead innocence through a defense of ignorance if liable to the charge of harboring her against my law.'

"As she says this she hands him a flyer containing Psyche's name and everything else. And after she does that she rushes off *6.8*   straightaway for home. Nor did Mercury fail to follow her orders. You see, in the mouths of all the people of every nation, running here and there far and wide, here is how he fulfilled his obligation, the cry that he was bid to cry:

"'Whoever can bring the runaway back in, or can reveal where the runaway is hidden—the king's daughter, the handmaiden of Venus, Psyche by name—may come to the shrine of Murtia, behind the south turn in the Circus Maximus; may meet Mercury, the town crier; may receive from Venus herself, under the guise of payment for such information, seven sweet kisses, and one made far more honeyed by the deep press of the caress of her tongue.'

Venus and Psyche

"Because Mercury made his public pronouncement in this way, cupidity for such a reward pricked up the interest of all mortals everywhere, each striving to outdo the other. And that is what, at this particular moment, removed all Psyche's reluctance and irresolution. And so, as she walks up to the doors of her good mistress, one of Venus' domestic staff, Convention by name, crosses her path and instantly cries out, as loud as she can:

"'Finally! The lowly handmaiden, the last word in loathsomeness—you've just begun to understand that you have a good mistress? Or could it be, in line with the insolence of the rest of your manners, that this too is part of your make-believe, that you don't know what great labors and pains we have undertaken in all our searches for you? Lucky for you that you fell into my hands and no one else's—that you find yourself stuck in the very claws of Hell—but you will pay the price, and on the double, don't you know, for such brazen, overbearing behavior.'

"She then made bold to lay hands on her hair and to drag her inside; Psyche resisted not at all. And as soon as Venus catches sight of Psyche, now brought before her and laid at her feet, she bursts into wide-mouthed laughter, the sort that the violent and angry make; then she shakes her head; then she tugs at her right ear, and says:

6.9

"'Finally! So you've condescended to pay a call on your mother-in-law? Or is it your husband you've come to visit instead, at death's door from the trauma you inflicted? But please! Don't worry yourself; I'll receive you now as a good daughter-in-law ought to be received.'

"Then she said, 'Where are my handmaidens, Anxiety and Melancholy?'

"They were brought in, and Venus handed her over to them to be tortured. They followed their lady's command: they scourged poor little Psyche with the cat-o'-nine-tails; they harrowed her with their other instruments of torment; and then they bring her back in again to their good mistress' presence. Once more Venus bursts out laughing.

"'Well would you look at this!' she says. 'She tries to inspire my pity by the appeal of her swelling belly, that she would make me a blessèd grandmother, don't you know, by her glorious

offspring! So this would put me on cloud nine, to be called grandmother when in the flower and vigor of my age, to have the son
of some cheap handmaiden called Venus' grandson? Though I am
a fool to use the empty name of son: this is not a marriage but a
misalliance and, what's more, contracted as it was in the country,
without witnesses, and without his father's consent, the marriage
cannot be considered legitimate. Therefore it shall be born a bas-
tard if, that is, I'll allow you to bring the birth to term at all.'

Psyche's First Trials

6.10   "Her prophecy pronounced, Venus flies at Psyche: she rips her
clothes to scraps and shreds, tears her hair out in clumps, gives
her head a good pummeling, drubs her disgracefully; then she
takes grains of wheat and barley and millet, poppy seeds and
chickpeas and lentils and beans, jumbles them all together and
mounds them up, mixes them together in one big heap, and here
is what she says to her:

"'Now as it seems to me that you, my misshapen handmaiden,
only win the good graces of your lovers by your ceaseless service
and nothing else, I am now going to test the goodness of your
grain myself. Sort out this mass and disarray of seeds, and when
every individual grain has been properly separated and assigned,
submit your completed work to me for my approval—and by this
very evening.'

"The pile of seeds—so many, so vast—was left in Psyche's care,
and Venus went off to some wedding feast. Now Psyche does not
even put a hand to that mass of confusion, that labyrinth, but,
flummoxed by the enormity of her enormous demand, she falls
into drop-jawed silence. But then an ant—that Lilliputian lover of
the countryside—ascertained the scale of the difficulty involved,
took pity on the menial labor of the woman who shared the great
god's bed, and cursed the sadistic cruelty of the mother-in-law.
He runs here and there and without hesitation calls together,
summons into assembly, all the troops of the ants from the surrounding areas.

"'*Misericordia!* Have pity, all you light-footed nurslings of
Earth, Mother of All! Have pity and with all the speed you can

manage run to the aid of the wife of Love, the elegant little girl who is now at death's door.'

"Waves of the six-footed nations spill in, and other waves after those, and each group with the utmost, earnest effort goes through the whole mound grain by grain. After each species of seed is divided out and set apart, they all disappear from sight in the twinkling of an eye.

"But Venus comes back at nightfall from her wedding banquet, dripping with wine, fragrant with unguent and balsam, all her body wrapped in wreaths of glistening roses, and she observes the meticulous accomplishment of this miraculous effort. *6.11*

"'This is not your work,' she says, 'my loathsome and foul handmaiden, not the work of your hands but his—and it is to your grief, and his as well, that you have found favor with him!'

"She throws a crust of bread, slave rations, at her feet and then goes off to bed. In the meanwhile, Cupid was in solitary confinement, under close watch, shut in a one-room apartment in the interior of the house, partly so that he couldn't make his wound the worse through his immodest and sensuous obsessions, partly so that he couldn't arrange an assignation with his heart's desire. So this is the way the two lovers drained a dreadful night to the dregs, torn asunder and kept apart while under the same roof. But just as Aurora came riding up on her horses, Psyche was summoned and thus spake Venus:

"'Do you see that grove, the one that extends along the length of the bank of the river flowing past, and the bushes in its depths that look down onto the companion spring? There are sheep that amble there, grazing unshepherded; blossoming on their backs is a true glory, gold that shines like the sun. I would recommend that you bring back to me posthaste a tuft of the strands of this precious fleece, gotten in whatever way you can.'

"So Psyche set out, and of her own free will, but no, not intending to fulfill her orders but to find rest and release from her misfortunes in a suicide leap from a rock at the river's edge. But then from the river there comes a heaven-sent sweet breath blowing in a soft rustle, and the green marsh-reed, patron and provider of mellifluous music, offers this prophecy: *6.12*

"'O Psyche, trained in trial and tribulation, no! Do not pollute my sacred waters by your pathetic and pitiable death! Nor is this the right time for you to assay a foray against those sinister sheep. So long as they catch and keep the heat from the scorching sun they are savage, vicious, rabid, mad: with horns sharp for goring and heads rock-hard for butting, they often take sadistic delight in the death and destruction of mortal men, and their bite is poison. However, until the fires of the noonday sun are banked, until these beasts simmer down in the cool calm of the river breeze, you can hide yourself out of sight beneath that towering tall sycamore that drinks with me simultaneously the same river current. And then, just as soon as their madness is mitigated, when they let go their anger and drop their guard, if you shake the branches of the grove nearby you will find your wooly gold, for it clings to the bushes that are grown dense together, everywhere you look.'

6.13   "In this way the straight and straightforward reed, humane and compassionate, taught suffering, heart-sick Psyche the path of her salvation. She gave ear and did not regret it; she took instruction and was not reckless; she did not fail. Every rule is carefully kept, and in light-fingered larceny she brings herself back to Venus with the folds of her gown full of the softness of this shining gold. But for all that, the risk of this her second task did not earn her any seconding approval; at least, not from her good mistress. No, but Venus from beneath her beetling brows smiled an acrimonious smile, and here is what she said:

"'That counterfeit agent, that Casanova—it does not escape me that he is the doer of this deed too. But now I shall make careful trial and see whether you and you alone are endowed with a brave heart and unprecedented providence. Do you see the peak of that steep mountain that towers over that soaring rock? How from that peak the sable waters cascade from the black spring? How those waters are dammed in the reservoir of the adjacent valley, then flood the marshes of the River Styx, then feed the loud-roaring waters of Cocytus? Take this little bottle and bring it back to me posthaste—full of the ice-cold water drawn from the bubbling depths of that loftiest spring.'

"And as she said this she handed over to Psyche a vessel carved out of crystal, and some still sterner admonitions in addition.
6.14   And off Psyche goes; she puts on some speed, keen and zealous, seeking the very summit of the mountaintop, expecting at least to find there the end of her awful and luckless life. But just as soon as she draws close to the mountain reaches near the cliff that Venus had spoken of, she realizes the death-dealing difficulty of her enormous endeavor. There was the upthrust of the rock in its

massive proportions, offering no firm foothold in its unscalable irregularity; from the middle of its jaws of stone shot torrents of the awful waters, and they, released from the hollows of its down-sloping passages, cascading down the sheer rock face, were confined within walls of a narrow channel that they had carved for themselves, then fell invisibly into the adjacent valley below. What should she see to the left and the right of the spring but sadistic serpents slithering out of hollows in the rock, their eyes in the service of their unblinking sentry duty, the pupils of their eyes in sleepless vigilance, endlessly open in ceaseless sight. And now the very waters were singing out, seeking to protect themselves. For they cry out forever and a day *Go back!* and *What do you think you're doing? Watch out!* and *What are you up to? Look out!* and *Run away!* and *You are going to die!* And so it was that Psyche herself turned to stone from the sheer impossibility of it all; though present in body she was absent in sense; absolutely buried by the burden of this labyrinth of danger, she had no recourse even to crying, the consolation that comes at the end of one's rope.

"But the agony of this simple and sinless soul did not escape the notice of the profound gaze of good mistress Providence. For all at once that royal bird, the eagle of Jupiter the most high, the claws that catch, spread its wings on its left and its right and appeared in her presence. He remembered the favor that Cupid had done him of old when, following Cupid's lead, he had stolen away for Jupiter from Phrygia his new cup-bearer Ganymede; now he was bringing Cupid help in the nick of time. Dancing attendance on Cupid and his power at the time of his wife's labors, the eagle abandons Jupiter's pathways at the zenith of heaven, swoops down, and perches before the girl, face to face. He begins:

6.15

"'You're a simple girl—it's your nature—and for such things as these you have no particular knowledge either. Do you really expect that you can steal away even a single drop from this fountain—holy, yes, and numinous, but perilous and treacherous—or even put a finger in it? If only by rumor, you've surely discovered that the waters of the Styx strike fear even into the gods, even Jupiter himself; the oaths that you mortals swear by the power of the gods the gods themselves swear by the august authority of the Styx. So give me your little bottle.'

"He snatches it straightaway, clutches it in his claws and shoots off; keeping their massive might in equipoise as they dipped to one side and the other he guided the oarage of his wings to the left and the right, between the dragons' dens—their jaws with the sadistic teeth, the elongations of their triple-forked tongues—and extracted the waters, though they defied him, though they threatened him, that he should fly away before any harm came to him. He told them a lie: he was under Venus' orders to get the water and had submitted himself to her service, and this made for just

6.16   a little more ease of access in his approach. And so the little bottle was filled and Psyche joyfully caught it and took it back to Venus at a run.

Psyche in the Underworld

"But for all that she was not able even then to placate the power and the prejudice of the sadistic goddess. For here is how Venus threatens her with greater and worse degradations; she calls her to her side and smiles a smile of death and destruction:

"'So you must be some sort of witch—I really do think so—a great witch of the great abyss, you who obeyed all these orders of mine without hesitation. But you'll still be obliged, honey child, to perform for me this one remaining task. Take this little jar'— she handed it to her—'and train your steps straightaway to the Land of the Dead and the hellish hearth and home of Orcus himself. Then hand the jar over to Proserpina. "Venus has a request," you'll say: "could you send her a little bit of your beauty, perhaps just enough for one brief, little day? For the beauty that she had she has spent completely, worn away utterly, while playing the nursemaid to her sick little son." But you get back here quick and no dawdling—I'll be putting in an appearance in the theater of the gods, and *that* is the makeup I must put on first.'

6.17   "And it was at that very moment that Psyche realized that her luck had run out. The veil was parted and she saw without a shadow of a doubt that she was being marched to her instant annihilation. And why not? She was being forced to journey on her own two feet and under her own power to Tartarus and the dear departed dead. She hesitates no longer. She hurries off to a towering tower, intending to throw herself from it headlong, for she reckoned that that way she could descend to the Land of the Dead quickly, sweetly, and neatly. But the tower bursts forth into un-expected voice.

"'You poor little girl!' it said. 'Why are you trying to snuff your-self out in this suicide leap? Why collapse so carelessly now at this task, at the finish line of your perils? If your breath is sepa-rated from your body one time, then yes, without any doubt, you will go to the depths of Tartarus, but you will not be able to return from there, not at all. Now you listen to me. Located not far from here is Sparta, the preeminent city of Achaea. Look for Taenarus there; it shares a border, but is hidden in trackless wilderness. There are the vents of Hell, and through the gaping jaws of its portal you can glimpse the impassable path; as soon as you have stepped across its threshold and entrusted yourself to its custody you will proceed by a direct and well-trammeled route to the very palace of Orcus himself.

6.18

"'But you'll be obliged not to walk through those shadows, not even that far, empty-handed. No; you'll need to carry cakes of barley meal, sops soaked thick with honey, in both your hands, and keep *two* coins with you in your mouth. And when a pretty part of your deadly journey is over you will come across a lame and limping ass with a burden of branches on his back; the ass-driver will be lame as well, and will ask you to hand him a few sticks that are falling from the load—produce not a single sound, but pass him by in silence. There will be no delay: you'll come then to the River of the Dead. Charon is in charge here, and will straightaway demand his ferry-fee; only then does he escort his voyagers to the farther shore on his raft of skins and patches. So miserliness lives and thrives even among the dead, and Charon, Hell's toll collector, that great god, does not do anything for nothing. No; the poor as they die must look for travel money, and should it happen that they don't have the cash to hand, no one will let them pass on. You will give this foul and filthy old man one of the two coins that you are keeping—you may call it your fare—but only on the condition that he take it up himself from your mouth with his own hand. And here too it will be no different: as you pass over this stagnant stream, an old man, a dead man, will be swimming on the surface; he will stretch out to you his moldering hands; he will beg you to draw him up into the boat. But for all that don't you be swayed by feelings of decency and duty: such feelings are prohibited.

6.19   "'Once the river has been crossed and you have traveled on a little way, old women, weavers setting up their loom, will beg you to lend them a hand, just for a moment; but for all that you are barred from even touching it. For all these obstacles and yet many others will rise up before you: their source is Venus' treachery, and her goal is to make you drop only one of the cakes from your hands. Please, don't think that an insignificant barley cake is an inconsequential loss. For if one of them be destroyed, this daylight will be denied you from that moment on. For there is a dog, an enormous one, endowed with a triptych of titanic heads, overpowering, horrifying; the barking that blasts from his jaws is like thunder over the dead—but he cannot hurt them now. Molesting them with meaningless menace, he is the eternal sentry before the threshold and the smoke-black halls of Proserpina, and guards the empty house of Hell. And you will pass by him easily, muzzled by the treat of one of your cakes; you will then go straightaway into the presence of Proserpina herself. She will receive you as a friend and with kindness, and her goal is to have you sit on her soft cushions and eat from her lavish and extravagant feast. Don't you do it. Sit on the ground; ask for coarse bread and eat that. Then announce to her the reason that you have come and take what is offered you; *then,* as you work your way back again, bribe that sadistic dog with the remaining barley cake; *then* give the greedy boatman the coin that you have kept in reserve. Once you have recrossed his river and retraced your earlier footsteps, you will return to this chorus, the heavenly stars in their courses. But of all my instructions, this I would recommend that you follow most particularly: don't even *want* to open or look into the jar that you are carrying; don't go sticking your nose in and trying for yourself this hidden treasure-store of divine beauty.'

6.20   "And that is how that commanding tower fulfilled its task of prophetic command. Psyche does not delay. She hurries off to Taenarus and properly prepares herself with the coins and the cakes; she runs down the path of the dead; she noiselessly passes by the limping donkey-driver; she gives the coin for river passage to the boatman; she disregards the desires of the dead man swimming; disdains the deceitful prayers of the women weaving; soothes to sleep the dog's blood-curdling madness with the ration of a barley cake; enters the house of Proserpina. Her hostess offered but Psyche did not accept her sumptuous seat and her blessèd food; she sat on the ground at Proserpina's feet and made do with the bread, slave's rations; she laid before her Venus' diplomatic commission. The jar was instantly filled and stoppered in secret; Psyche then takes it up and takes it away; she bars shut the jaws of the barking dog through the trick of the second barley cake; she hands over the leftover coin to the boatman and runs back up from the dead at a far livelier pace. She wins her way back to the bright daylight, and offers it her prayer of thanks, but, although she is hurrying to bring her orders to their ordained end, her mind is blinded by her reckless desire to stick her nose in.

"'Would you look at this!' she says. 'I am a fool! To be a courier for the beauty divine and not to abstract even a tiny little bit for myself from it, thus the more to please my own beautiful lover?'

"And with this word she opens up the bottle. But there is not a single thing in it, nor any beauty, but only the sleep of the dead, the incontrovertibly Stygian sleep. And instantly brought to light by the removal of the stopper it lays siege to her, pours itself over every one of her limbs in a coagulated and comatose cloud; Psyche is stopped in her tracks, falls to the ground on the path, and it takes possession of her. And so she lay there, unable to move, nothing more than a sleeping corpse.

6.21

Cupid to the Rescue

"But Cupid's wound is now scabbed over. As he regains his strength he can no longer endure the prolonged absence of his Psyche. He slips out of the window, high above in the wall in the room in which he had been imprisoned, and on wings now recovered after his considerable rest he flies forward at a far faster pace. He rushes to his Psyche. Thoroughly and thoughtfully he daubs the sleep away and restores it to its original home inside the bottle; he rouses his Psyche with the point of his arrow, and it does not harm her.

"'Would you look at this!' he said. 'You'd lost your life again, poor little girl, sticking your nose in, just as before. But in the meanwhile, you really must bring to completion without hesitation the mission that was enjoined upon you at my mother's command; and I—I will see to everything else.'

"After he said that, the flighty lover lifted himself lightly on his wings: Psyche, on the other hand, brings back to Venus posthaste the present that Proserpina had proffered.

6.22   "In the meantime, Cupid is deathly afraid of his mother's sudden conversion to abstinence, for he is eaten alive by his inordinate love, and has the love-sick look to prove it. So now he's back to his old tricks. On wings swift as the wind he forces his way into the heights of heaven; he places himself before great Jupiter as a suppliant and argues his case. Then Jupiter lays hold of Cupid's cherubic cheek, draws hand and cheek to his mouth, and kisses him. Here is how he speaks to him:

"'My boy, good sir, despite the fact that you have never defended the dignity that is decreed to me by the authorization of the gods—oh no! YOU have shot at me again and again and pierced the heart within my breast which would arrange the balance of the four elements and the risings and the settings of the stars; have besmirched it in uncountable instances of land-bound lust; have, in defiance of the laws—the *lex Julia* on adultery in particular—and public decency, destroyed my reputation and my good name in foul affairs and fornications, miserably metamorphosing my august aspect and calm countenance into serpents, into flames, into the beasts of the wild, the birds of the air, the livestock of the barnyard—for all that, I say, I still remember my mild and modest manner, and that you grew up cradled in the palm of my hand. I will do all that you ask. But there is one proviso: you must learn to look out for your rivals and, if there is somewhere on earth a girl who truly surpasses all the others in beauty, she is how you must pay me back for the favor I'm doing you now, *quid pro quo*.'

6.23   "Thus spake Jupiter. He orders Mercury to call all the gods into council straightaway, and to make a proclamation that whoever is absent from the heavenly assembly will be fined ten thousand *sesterces* as a punishment. From fear of *that* the heavenly theater is instantly filled and Jupiter, head and shoulders above them all, sitting on his throne on high, makes this pronouncement:

"'You gods whose names are inscribed in the roll book of the Muses, you supernal senators, you all know this young man, no doubt, and how I reared and raised him with these my hands. I have determined that the ardent, amorous impulses of his incipient adolescence need to be reined in by some bridle; it is enough that he has been slandered and slurred by daily defamations of adultery and every other kind of debauchery. Every opportunity must be taken from him; every youthful sensuous extravagance must be bound by the bridal ball and chain. He has taken himself a mortal girl, and taken her virginity too; let him keep her, to have and to hold; let him embrace his Psyche and enjoy his love forever.'

Reconciliation and Lawful Marriage

"Then he turns his face toward Venus.

"'Daughter of mine,' he said, "don't be sad, not at all; have no fear for your ancient nativity or your glorious pedigree or for the social standing deriving from this mortal marriage. For I shall so work my will that this will be not a misalliance but a marriage, legitimate and conforming to the code of civil law.'

"And right then and there he gives the order through Mercury that Psyche is to be snatched up and brought up into heaven. He offers her a goblet of ambrosia from his outstretched arm.

"'Take this, Psyche,' he says, 'and be immortal. Cupid shall never stray from his bond to you; no—this marriage shall endure forever for you both.'

"There is no delay. Doors open onto a wedding banquet where the fine food was flowing freely. The groom lay on the couch of honor, his Psyche in his embrace; Jupiter with his Juno likewise; and then came all the other gods in descending order. Jupiter's own cup-bearer, that mortal boy from the Trojan countryside, offered him a cup of nectar; Liber offered a cup to all the rest; Vulcan cooked the dinner; the Hours with flowers, roses and others, turned everything to royal red and purple; the Graces sprinkled balsam and perfume. There was music too: the Muses made the hall echo with melody and harmony; Apollo sang a song to the lyre; beautiful Venus came in on cue to the sweet music and danced, in a stage scene so artfully orchestrated that the Muses sang as chorus or played the double-flute, and a Satyr and a Son-of-Pan warbled to a shepherd's pipe. And that was how Psyche was joined in legitimate marriage to Cupid; and there is born to them in the fullness of term and time a *daughter*—our name for her is Delight."

6.24

The Audience Escapes

6.25   And that was the story that the old crone told, in her drunkenness and delirium, to the captive and captivated girl. And I—standing off to one side, not too far away—I was in anguish, believe you me, because I had neither steno books nor stylus to record such a beguiling fiction.

But then, whom should I see but the robbers arriving with their arms full; some furious fight had been fought and finished, yet a fair number of them—the more eager ones, in fact—were impatient to leave the injured behind to lick their wounds and to set out again for the remaining bags and bales that they had hidden, as they kept on saying, in a cave. And so they hurry their breakfast and bolt their food; they take their cudgels and wallop us with them, my horse and me, who were to be the conveyance for all those things; they lead us out into the road. Then they lead us all the way, by the eve of the day, to some cave; we were bone-weary after all the hills and all the twists and turns. And from there, without so much as the briefest break, not refreshed and not revived, they lead us back again, quick march, laden with many things indeed; and they kept goading us on in such anxiety and apprehension that, as they were walloping me onward, stroke on stroke and blow on blow, driving me forward, they forced me to stumble over a rock that was lodged in place along the side of the road. It is only with difficulty that they can force me to get back up again from there, maimed as I was in a right leg and a left hoof, because of all the beatings they'd just assailed me with, just as they had at the outset.

6.26   And one of them says: "How much longer, and to what good purpose, shall we feed and keep this broken-backed ass, now lame to boot?"

Another says: "And what of the fact that he came to our hideout left foot first? From that ill-omened moment on we have taken no proper profit at all, only blood and trauma and the slaughterings of our bravest men."

Yet another chimes in: "Well, as for me—make no mistake—unwilling though he may be, as soon as he's carried these bales and bundles back for us, I'm going to pitch him straightaway off a cliff, to make him a meal that the vultures will find exactly to their taste."

And while these gentlemen, most meek and mild, were talking my death back and forth amongst themselves, we had actually arrived back home. My fear, you see, had turned my hooves into wings. Then in a hurry they off-loaded the burdens we bore, without a care or a concern either for our salvation or even for my death; they went to get their friends, the wounded ones who had stayed behind all this time, and came running back out intending to fetch the rest of the things themselves, out of impatience, as they kept on saying, at our shiftlessness and indolence. Yet for all that there was no small stone in my hoof aggravating me as I contemplated the death that now threatened me, and I had this conversation with myself:

"Lucius! Why are you standing still? What else is it that you *think* will happen at the end of the line? Death—a most bitter and untimely death—has been planned for you; the robbers have decreed it. And this plan of theirs requires no very great effort. Do you see those jagged rocks so close to you, the razor-sharp flints that stick up out of them? They'll run you through, and before you hit the ground they will tear you to pieces, limb from limb. And another thing: that magic of yours, that radiant magic, gave you only the face of an ass and the burdens of an ass; it didn't wrap around you the thick hide of an ass, but only the tender tissues of a leech.

"I know: why don't you finally wrap a man's courage around you and look out for your own salvation while you have the chance? The opportunity that you have for a getaway will never be better, so long as the robbers are gone. Surely you won't be afraid of the watch kept by this half-dead old woman? You could end her life with a single kick of your hoof, even if your leg is lame. But where in this whole wide world could an ass make a getaway to? Who would offer him sanctuary? But this is a very stupid question and an absolutely asinine thought—after all, who would walk along the road and not gladly take him away as a mount he could ride on himself?"

And instantly, with a swift and sudden tug, I snap the lash that I had been hitched with and I bolt forwards at a four-footed gallop. Yet that old woman was pretty sharp; she had the eyes of a vulture and I couldn't escape them. You see, as soon as she catches sight of me freed from my tether, she conceives of a boldness that exceeds her sex and her age: she lays hold of the lash and tries hard to turn me around and call me back. And I—well, 6.27

for all that, remembering as I did the robber's decree of death and destruction, I am not moved by any feeling of human decency, none at all. No, I strike out at her with kicks from my hind feet and knock her straightaway to the ground with a resounding thud. And she—well, even though she had been knocked flat to the ground, she kept that lash laced tight around her with an iron grip. The result? She trailed along behind me for a short time, dragged in dust as I ran on ahead.

And instantly she starts in crying out for the aid of some stronger hand in strident, raucous ululations. But her weeping and wailing were unavailing, and she was trying to sound an alarm to no purpose, inasmuch as there was no one there who could bring her any aid or assistance; no one, that is, but that lone captive maiden. She comes running out at the invitation of her voice and sees, by Hercules, a spectacle, a Theban tragic scene of noteworthy novelty: an agèd Dirce dragging not behind a bull but an ass. The girl takes on the unflinching bravery of a man and dares a deed that was very pretty indeed, for she unwraps the lash from the old woman's hands, calls me back from my onrush with words murmured in a soft hush, climbs up on my back without hesitation and in this way spurs me on again to a run.

6.28   And I made the hard ground echo at a four-footed gallop, at a race-horse pace, both from my selfish desire for my own getaway and from my heroic enthusiasm for freeing the girl—but also from the encouraging flicks of her whip, which kept urging me on, more often than *strictly* necessary. I kept trying to whinny in response to the light and lovely words that came from the maiden's mouth. And in fact, while pretending to scratch my own back, I would now and again bend my neck backwards and try to kiss the girl's delectable feet. And then she drew up a sigh from deep down within, and turned toward heaven with apprehensive eyes:

"You gods above!" she said. "Now, at last, come to my aid in the depths of my danger! And you, too inflexible Fortune, now cease your sadistic attacks! Enough of my blood has been spilled on your altar from these crucifixions of mine. And *you*—the fortress of my liberation and my salvation—if you can deliver me home safe and sound to my mother and father, if you can give me back to my beautiful fiancé, how great will be the thanks I'll render, how great will be the honors I'll offer, how great will be the food I'll set before you! And first of all I'll dress this mane of yours: I'll decorate it right and proper with the jewelry of my maidenhood; your forelock I'll curl first and then I'll part it prettily; the rough hairs of your tail, tangled and matted through long disregard of daily bathing, I'll restore to their proper luster, curried and combed out with care. You will shine like the stars of the night sky, studded with chains and medallions, in abundance and made of gold; you will march in triumph to the rejoicing of the people who will parade alongside you; and I will stuff you full every day with the nuts and yet more delicate treats that I will carry in the folds of my silken gown—you, my savior.

"But you will not just live in the lap of luxury and leisure, delighting in delectable foods, one blessèd day after another; glory and honor will be yours as well. You see, I will set my seal upon the memory of my present good fortune and of divine Providence herself in a testament that will last forever: I will dedicate in the atrium of my house a representation of my present getaway, painted on a proper board. A simple story, but it shall be seen; it shall be retold in travelers' tales; it shall endure forever on the pens of learnèd authors: *The Princess Bride Escaping from Bondage on the Back of an Ass*. And you yourself will join the lists of the wonders of ancient days, and we will all believe by the example of your honest truth that Phrixus *did* swim the Hellespont on the back of a ram, that Arion *was* a dolphin's charioteer, that Europa *did* lie on the back of a bull. And if it is true that Jupiter bellowed like a bull, then it could be that in the ass that saved me there lies lurking a human face, or even the visage of a god!"

6.29

And while the girl was rolling and unrolling this scroll, again and again, interleaving her unending sighing with her prayers, we came to where three roads met, and there she grabbed my halter and was impatiently and vigorously trying to get me to direct my steps to the right, because that was the path, I supposed, that led to her mother and father. But I was well aware that the robbers had gone that way to get the rest of the loot, so I dug in and kept fighting back, and here is how I tried to state my grievance in the silence of my mind:

"What do you think you're doing, you luckless girl? What are you up to? Why are you hurrying off to Hell? And why are you trying to do it on *my* legs? It's not only yourself, you know, but me as well, that you're going to do in."

The Death of the Storyteller

And so we were pulling in opposite directions, and found ourselves in a dispute over some property line, over the ownership of the earth at our feet, trying to divide the road, whether she would go her way or I would go mine, when the robbers, their arms full of the loot they'd taken, catch us in the act; they'd already recognized us from a long way off by the bright light of the moon, and they greet us with a wicked smile. And here is how one of their number calls us out:

6.30

"Where are you off to, traveling this ribbon of moonlight with such haste to your pace? It's the dead of night—have you no fear of ghouls and ghosts? Could it be that you, you most virtuous girl, were hurrying to some clandestine rendezvous with your mother and father? No; *we'll* be your fortress in the wilderness, and *we'll* show you a good shortcut to you and yours."

And another follows that phrase with his fist. He lays hold of my lash and twists me around backwards and with his accustomed cudgelings he hardly spares the rod that he carried with him, the one with the knots and the knobs. So I'm *running* back to the death that is waiting for me, but against my will; then I remember my anguished hoof and start in to limp, my head bobbing up and down. But the man who had dragged me back said, "Well, look here! Reeling like a drunken man again, stumbling and staggering? Those rotten feet of yours—they know how to run away but they don't know how to walk? And just a short time before now the speed of wingèd Pegasus was no match for you!"

While my generous friend was joking with me this way, always with a flourish of his club, we had reached the outer palisades of their hideout, and imagine this, if you will: the old woman had put a noose around her neck and was hanging from a branch of a towering cypress tree. They dragged her down straightaway and threw her headlong over a cliff, still tied with her own rope. The girl they immediately sequestered in chains and then, with the ferocity of wild animals, they lay siege to the dinner that the old woman had prepared for them with posthumous painstakingness.

Appendix I

Apuleius

On the God of Socrates 16

Apuleius considered himself to be a philosopher; or, better, like many another contemporary rhetorician, he considered philosophy a fitting topic for popular lectures. Viewed as a piece of display rhetoric, *On the God of Socrates* is quite at home in the Second Sophistic movement of the second century. But it is its philosophical underpinning that interests us here. Apuleius is a middle Platonist, and a peculiarity of middle Platonism is its well-developed demonology: *On the God of Socrates* is the fullest and most systematic account of this demonology preserved for us. There is a hierarchy of intermediary spirits between the human world and the ultimate reality that is the place of the origin of the soul. Socrates' divine sign, the *daimonion* who told him when he was about to do something wrong, but never when he was about to do something right, is swept up into this spirit-filled world. Consequently, Apuleius speaks of Socrates' *daimonion* practically as an individual guardian spirit. Plato's notion of a *daemon* as a guardian of the fate of an individual soul, as a sort of spirit-guide, here overwhelms the particularity of the voice of Socrates' own experience. In this passage, Apuleius specifically names Amor as one of these *daemones*, paired with its opposite Somnus (Sleep). To some extent, this suggests that Cupid in *Cupid and Psyche* may function as Psyche's guardian spirit, the spirit that wakes the soul up; but in other and obvious ways, Amor and Cupid are very different creatures.

Bibliography: The explosion of interest in Apuleius' *Golden Ass* has fortunately spilled over into his other works. There are two recent translations of *The God of Socrates* provided with introductions and notes that are the best starting point for further reading:

that of Stephen M. Trzaskoma in Calder et al. (2002, pp. 245–72; a reprint of Moreschini's Latin text follows, pp. 273–304) and that of S. J. Harrison in Harrison et al. (2001, pp. 185–216). For Apuleius' position in the history of middle Platonism, see Gersh (1986, pp. 215–328) and Dillon (1996, pp. 306–37). Rist (1963) is still a valuable starting point for understanding this later history of Socrates' *daimonion;* the most recent work on the *daimonion* is Partridge (2008). The text is that of Moreschini (1991), referred to by the now-traditional section number and page numbers of Oudendorp's 1823 edition.

XVI (154) But all of this division into categories pertained only to those *daemones* who were at one time contained within a human body. But there are others: not less in number, far more distinguished in honor, that higher, that more exalted class of *daemones* who were always free from the shackles and bonds of the human body and who are in charge of particular powers. Among their company are Somnus and Amor. (155) These have forces that are mutually exclusive: Amor, that of waking people up; Somnus, that of putting people to sleep. And so it is from this loftier abundance of *daemones* that Plato thinks that witnesses and guardians have been granted to human beings individually in the conduct of their lives;[1] never visible to anyone, they are to be perpetually present as judges, not only of every action performed but also of every thought conceived. But when life has been rendered up and one must return, that same *daemon,* who had been placed in charge of us, snatches (the soul) away instantly, drags it along to judgment as if it were its prisoner, and in that place stands by it for the pleading of its case: whatever lies it tells, to argue the opposite; whatever truths it tells, to corroborate; in fact, it is by its testimony that sentence is pronounced. And so, all of you, you who are listening to this divine conviction of Plato's through my intermediation, for whatever action you may do, for whatever thought you may contemplate, so educate your souls that you realize that there is nothing for any human being that is a secret from these guardians, neither within the mind nor outside of it.

1. Key passages are *Timaeus* 90a–d, *Phaedo* 107d–108c, and the end of *Republic* 617e–621d.

No; it shares in all things, sticking its nose in;[2] (156) it sees all things; it understands all things; it dwells in the very inner sanctum of the mind playing the role of the conscience. This *daemon* of whom I speak is one's unique guardian, one-and-only overseer, internal observer, exclusive custodian, intimate advocate, painstaking eyewitness, personalized judge, inescapable witness, a defender of what is good, a prosecutor of what is bad, and, so long as it is respectfully acknowledged, diligently appreciated, and conscientiously worshiped—just as it was worshiped by Socrates by means of his justice and his innocence—it looks ahead in unpredictable times, gives advance warning in unsettled times, a defender in times of trial, a preserver in times of want. It can now in dreams, now by signs, now perhaps even face to face when the situation demands it, ward off evil things from you, bring to fruition good things for you, raise up what is lowly, prop up what is unstable, light up what is dark, guide what is prosperity, set straight what is calamity.

2. Latin *curiose;* I keep the translation that was used throughout *The Golden Ass*.

Appendix II

Martianus Capella

The Marriage of Philology and Mercury I.7

Some time in the late fifth century (the 470s or 480s), Martianus Capella, a native of Roman Carthage, wrote an encyclopedia of the seven liberal arts that he cryptically presented as an allegory of the apotheosis of earthly wisdom: *The Marriage of Philology and Mercury*. But this wisdom, not the bloodless philology of book learning, is evidently code for theurgy, the knowledge of the divine world and of the words that can manipulate it, a "love of words" in a very particular sense. In the opening two books, Mercury searches for a bride, selects Philology, and then prepares her for her ascent to Olympus. In a crucial scene, she vomits forth her learning (2.135–39); only when thus unburdened does she have the ability to sense the ultimate reality, the Undefinable Father who lives outside of the universe and whom one may only address in mystic sounds, beyond the constraints of language-bound speech and discursive thought (2.200–5). Maidens representing the seven liberal arts collect the books that she has vomited and present them to her as wedding presents on Olympus, and thus the differences between divine wisdom and book learning, and between divinity itself and the world of the traditional Olympian gods, are made clear.

Martianus clearly knows his fellow countryman Apuleius. In many general ways, his account of marriage and apotheosis is inspired by *Cupid and Psyche* but is also a corrective to it. Here is how to speak of ascent to heaven in mystical, not erotic, terms, and the reader of *Cupid and Psyche* can see in this reaction to it just how gossamer-like is the intellectual substance of Psyche's tale in Apuleius. To Martianus, the tale *Cupid and Psyche* represents a fall, but the story of Mercury and Philology represents a true ascent. At the very beginning of the *Marriage*, we learn that Mercury's first three choices for a bride are all unavailable for various reasons: Sophia, Wisdom, is self-contemplative and not suited for union with another; Mantice, Prophecy, belongs to Apollo; Psyche has been abducted and held captive by Cupid. Philology proves to be both appropriate and available. Shanzer (1986) argues that the first three maidens represent different types of souls, and that Psyche is the innocent soul that falls because of sensual indulgence and thus needs to be redeemed. What the reader of *Cupid and Psyche* should notice here is that Martianus does not attempt to summarize Apuleius' tale; that he gives his own accounting, giving parents to Psyche and describing the presents the gods gave her on the day of her birth; that the fall of Psyche is clearly described as the descent of a soul from the place of its origins to the world of matter; that this allegory is fully detailed and represents an understanding of human nature that is crucial to Martianus' overall scheme; that both a Heavenly Venus and a Vulgar Venus are implied; that the goal of the soul is to overcome the darkness of matter, rediscover its origins, and travel by means of an astral body back to where it came from. Most important, what Cupid does to Psyche in Martianus is imprison her and keep her from returning; sexual Love represents Death and a fall into the world, whereas in Apuleius sexual Love represents the force that grants the soul immortality, and a symbolic death is a form of self-sacrifice that makes Psyche worthy.

In other words, this is not a simple reading of *Cupid and Psyche*; after all, as Plotinus says, there are many depictions of their relations, both in story and in art. Martianus may even be alluding to other philosophical accounts and not just referring to Apuleius, whom he does not name. While the Middle Ages could see the difference between Apuleius' story and Martianus' account, not everyone did. Boccaccio gave the names Sol and Endelechia to the parents of Psyche in his retelling and interpretation of *Cupid and Psyche* in his *Genealogies of the Pagan Gods* (5.22, "On Psyche, the fifteenth daughter of Apollo").

Bibliography: The starting point for any study of Martianus is Stahl et al. (1971); the only complete English translation is Stahl et al. (1977). Absolutely essential for understanding the intellectual and religious background of the allegory is Shanzer (1986), which includes a translation of Book 1 (pp. 202–19; this passage is on

p. 204). For Martianus Capella and Menippean satire see both
Shanzer (1986, 29–44) and Relihan (1993, 137–51). For another
translation of this passage and a good discussion of Martianus'
use of Apuleius in general, see Carver (2007, 36–40). For Boccaccio, see Gaisser (2008, 110–18) and Carver (2007, 133–41). The text
is that of Willis (1983), referred to by page and line number
(4.10–5.14).

[Mercury has just found Sophia unsuitable and Mantice unavailable.]

(4.10) He wanted then, if no one else, to ask for the hand of the
daughter of Endelichia[1] and Sol, for she was as beautiful as beautiful could be, and had been nurtured with extraordinary care by
all of the gods; for it was to this very Psyche that the gods brought
gift after gift when invited to a banquet on the day of her birth.
Jupiter, no less, had placed upon her head the crown that he had
taken off of Eternity, his own and favorite daughter; Juno added
as well a bridal band for her hair, derived from a radiant vein of
the most refined gold. (4.16) Even Tritonian Minerva loosened
Psyche's tunic, transferred her own breast band and her veil (like
flames they were, dyed in crimson), and, one virgin to another,
clothed her in the very mantle of her own wise and holy bosom.[2]
Delian Apollo as well, carrying as he was his laurel branch,
pointed out to her with this prognosticating and prophesying
wand the flights of birds, the bolts of lightning, and the paths of
the heaven itself and all of its stars. (4.20) On the other hand, the
gleaming mirror of Venus Urania, which Wisdom had affixed in
Urania's inner sanctum in among her other gifts, Urania with her
merciful generosity bestowed upon Psyche so that she could recognize herself and so come to learn to search out her own origin.
Lemnian Vulcan as well, the craftsman, lit for her flames of a
never-to-be-extinguished perpetuity, to keep her from being over-
whelmed by the gloom of shadows and the blindness of night.

1. Not Entelechia, as the text is sometimes emended. Entelechy refers to
a soul as a "fully actualised form of an organic body" (Shanzer 1986, 68);
endelechy refers to the soul's existence outside of a physical body.
2. This is the *aegis*, Athena's shield. These are Roman wedding preparations (particularly the ritual crimson veil, or *flammeum*) but with some
sort of symbolic twist: Psyche is being decked out in a sort of armor provided by a goddess who has no traditional association with marriage.

(4.24) But it was Aphrodite[3] who assigned all of her own enticements round about all of Psyche's senses; for she had slathered
her with oils and wreathed her round with flowers and then
taught her to be nourished and to be warmed by their scent; she
had seduced her with honey; she had persuaded her to gasp in
delight at gold and jeweled necklaces and to bind her limbs with
them in her pursuit of a supercilious superiority. And as Psyche
lay at rest, Aphrodite brought rattles to her and little bells, such
as she would use to put a baby to sleep. (5.5) And more than that,
to make certain that she did not pass any of her time away without enticement and excitement, she had assigned Delight[4] round
about the inmost parts of Psyche's body, tickling her with her intimate itch.

(5.7) But in fact it was Cyllenian Mercury himself who had presented her with a chariot[5] and swift wheels, so that she could run
this way and that with unbelievable speed, even though Memory
weighed her down, bound in shackles of gold.[6] So this was the
Psyche whom Arcadian Mercury, who had come away empty-
handed in his earlier attempts, wanted to take to wife, she who
had been made wealthy, been made rich, by these divine gifts,
who had been adorned by contribution after contribution of the
divinities of heaven. (5.11) But as it happened, Virtue was standing close by the side of Cyllenian Mercury, and she, practically
with tears in her eyes, announced that Psyche had been stolen
away from Virtue's company by the reckless passion of the god
with the quiver who flies, and that she was being held captive by
Cupid in adamantine chains.

3. Urania above had been translated as Venus Urania; this Aphrodite
then is Venus Pandemos.

4. Delight, *Voluptas*, is the name of Cupid and Psyche's daughter.

5. This refers to the astral body used by the soul in the heavens.

6. This is not the Platonic memory of the heavenly world such as one
would have expected in such a context, but evidently memory of earthly
and time-bound things, the enemy of ascent. Cf. *Phaedrus* 248c (trans.
Nehamas and Woodruff in Cooper 1997, 526): When the soul "by some
accident takes on a burden of forgetfulness and wrongdoing, then it is
weighed down, sheds its wings and falls to earth." Cf. also Psyche falling
back to earth after losing hold of Cupid at 5.24.

Appendix III

Fulgentius

The Mythologies III.6

The Tale of Psyche the Goddess and Cupid

In the middle of the sixth century, the Christian Fulgentius, also a Latin author from Africa, wrote a compendium of classical mythology, *Mythologies*, in three books. Its prologue is divided into three scenes and sets the tone: Calliope the Muse, with Satire and Urania in tow, arrives to stop the narrator from his revisionist plan to explain mythology away, to reveal its mystical kernel while rejecting its literal meanings; the creatures of myth are not to be dismissed as lightly as that. They take over the burden of explication from a narrator found at the end babbling in his sleep. Their tool is allegory, and they have a cavalier goal not so different from that of the narrator. They too will dispense with mythology as quickly as possible, but mythical creatures need to do the talking. The point is that there are no very great truths to be revealed here. A learned human exegete is not necessary and in fact seems comically out of place. It would seem that Calliope would present herself as an allegory when she explains away the Muses at 1.15, but the frame is largely forgotten after the prologue is over. The *Mythologies* can be contrasted to Fulgentius' *Allegorical Content of Vergil*, in which allegory reveals profound and Christian truths in the *Aeneid*; mythology, viewed as a set of stories without authors, gets in contrast a cursory treatment.

On the other hand, the story of *Cupid and Psyche* is singled out for special treatment. It is the longest section of the *Mythologies* and the only one that attempts to explain a specific literary text. In Fulgentius' Christian eyes, Psyche is punished for her desire.

(Psyche appears briefly in the prologue as well, as an example of one who lost what she loved by looking at it.) The reader should note how Calliope (or Fulgentius) leaves the second half of the story alone, providing very full detail only up to Psyche's banishment from Cupid's palace. The allegory is claimed to be obvious after only a few details. Fulgentius (to dispense with the fiction of the frame) does not in any way present a thorough reading or interpretation. He is mostly concerned with establishing the groundwork for an allegory: the king and queen are God and Matter; the daughters are Flesh, Free Will, and Soul. He has, in fact, very little patience, and it is interesting to see such an early proof of just how difficult it is to assign a specific allegorical value to the profusion of details in this story. Fulgentius is notorious as an inventor of sources, and Aristophontes of Athens, to whom he refers the reader who wants to know the details, is probably a convenient fiction; yet it too may suggest the existence of other written versions of a Cupid and Psyche story that are not Apuleius'.

Bibliography: The starting point for any study now of Fulgentius is Hays 1996. Hays also maintains a very full and annotated online bibliography of Fulgentian studies. His commentary with text and translation of the *Mythologies* and Fulgentius' other three authentic works is forthcoming from Oxford University Press. For the prologue as a Menippean satire, see Relihan 1993, 152–63. For Fulgentius' treatment of *Cupid and Psyche,* see Gaisser 2008, 53–58. See also Carver 2007, 41–47, for another translation (from a Renaissance, not a modern, edition) and analysis of this passage. The account of *Cupid and Psyche* in the so-called First Vatican Mythographer (written between 875 and 1075) is essentially the summary of the story provided by Fulgentius but without his allegorization; this is now available in English translation in Pepin 2008, 95–96. Fulgentius' Latin is tortured, inspired by the elaborateness of Apuleius' language. The text is quite unsound, and Hays' commentary will propose many changes. Any translation is therefore provisional in its details, even if it is clear in its general outlines. The text is that of Helm (1970) referred to by page and line number: 66.19–70.2.

(66.19) Within his *Metamorphoses* Apuleius spelled out this tale in no uncertain terms, when he said that there were, in a certain city, a king and a queen, and that they had three daughters. The two who were oldest were modest in appearance, while the youngest was of such glorious beauty that she was believed to be a Venus on earth. And so[1] marriages were contracted for the oldest two who were modest in appearance, but as for her, as if she were a goddess, there was no one who would dare to love her but was inclined to[2] worship her instead, begging her favor with sacrificial offerings. Therefore Venus, because the glory of the reverence due to her was diluted and polluted, burned with envy and called upon Cupid, to have him exact a strict punishment for such obnoxious beauty. Cupid came to avenge his mother but, when he saw the girl, he fell desperately in love with her, for the affliction was turned into affection and he, glorious bow-and-arrow man though he was, struck himself with his own weapon.

(67.9) And so it is that the girl, by the oracular pronouncement of Apollo, is commanded to be left alone on a mountaintop—led to the grave as it were in funereal rites of mourning and assigned to a husband who is a wingèd serpent. And now, the funeral procession duly concluded, the girl is carried down the steep slopes of the mountain by the gentle conveyance of the breath of the West Wind and is hustled away into a house of gold. Words of praise would be inadequate: this house, precious and priceless,[3] could only be appreciated by gazing upon it, and there, with voices and voices only in attendance upon her, she found herself in association with a spouse that was unrevealed, who came and went. For her husband would arrive at night and, when the battles of Venus had been fought to their conclusion in the shadows, just as he had come in the evening invisibly, just so did he depart as well in the morning unknown.

(67.19) And so it was that her servants were voices, and she was the lady of an ethereal house; but her intercourse was nocturnal, and unknown was her spouse.[4]

---

1. *denique*. In *The Golden Ass*, this is often translated "case in point," but it has a less definite sense here.

2. *pronus*. In *The Golden Ass*, this would have the implication of "falling on one's face," but is weaker here.

3. *pretiosa sine pretio*. This mimics Apuleius' phrase at 5.1, *sine pretio pretiosae*.

4. Fulgentius here aims for an Apuleian sort of jingle, which the translation approximates: *habuit ergo vocale servitium, ventosum dominium, nocturnum commercium, ignotum coniugium.*

(67.21) But her sisters come to weep for the death of this girl and, after they climb to the top of the mountain, they keep on calling out in a mournful voice that sisterly syllable. And although that light-shunning husband threatened her and forbade her the sight of her sisters, nevertheless the unconquerable urgency of the love of the ties of blood overshadowed the conjugal commandment. And so, by the huffing and puffing conveyance of the blowing breeze of the West Wind she brings to herself these sisterly relations and then, giving in to their poisoned plottings as regards the ascertaining of her husband's shape and form, she snatched up her desire to stick her nose in, a desire that played the wicked stepmother to her own salvation; putting the assistance that caution could bring behind her, she girds[5] herself as well with that most easy-going gullibility that is ever the mother of lies and deceit. And so, believing her sisters when they said that she was married to a serpent for a husband, she hides a razor under her pillow, intending to kill him as if he were a wild beast; an oil lamp she places under a basket as well. And when her husband was sleeping his deep, deep sleep, she armed herself with her weapon and, when she learned from the lamp that she unearthed from the protection of its basket that it was Cupid, she, being seared by the brazen solicitudes of love, burns her husband with the splattering of the bubbling lamp oil. Cupid escapes and, heaping reproach upon reproach upon the girl for sticking her nose in, he abandons her, an exile, banished from home. At length, after she has been tossed back and forth in Venus' many malicious maltreatments, he takes her afterwards in marriage with the sponsorship of Jupiter.[6]

(68.16) In fact, I could in this work have run through the whole sequence of the events of the tale—how she descended to the Underworld, how she filled her little bottle from the waters of the Styx, how she robbed the sheep of the Sun of their fleece, how she

---

5. Reading *accingit* with Hays for *arripit*, an erroneous repetition of *arripuit* earlier in the sentence, translated "snatched up." The image is military, snatching up a weapon (here, *curiositas*) and girding oneself with armor (here, *credulitas*).

6. "With the sponsorship of Jupiter": There is something wrong with the text here. Editions print *Iove petente*, "at the request of Jupiter," which misunderstands Apuleius. The translation provides an approximation of what seems to be the required sense.

sorted out the jumbled grains of seeds, how she took a little bit of
Proserpina's beauty and was about to die—but both because
Apuleius has related nothing but[7] a mass of lies in prolific detail,
practically filling two of his chapters, and because Aristophontes
of Athens, in his books called †disaristeia†,[8] has laid this tale out
for those who long to learn it in an interminable roundabout of
words, we have decided for this reason that it is wholly super-
fluous to put in our books material that has been laid out by
others, so as not to banish our efforts beyond the bounds of their
proper competence or to involve them in enterprises that are not
their own.

(69.2) But since the reader of this tale is turning to these analy-
ses of ours in order to find out what the lies of those other books
mean—The city they employed to symbolize, as it were, the
World; in it they employed the king and queen to symbolize God
and Matter. To them they add three daughters: that is, Flesh, Au-
tonomy (what we call Freedom of the Will), and Soul. For in
Greek Soul is called Psyche, and they wanted her to be the
youngest for this reason, because they used to say that the soul is
inserted afterwards into a body already made; and she is therefore most beautiful for this reason, that she is more elevated than
freedom and more honorable than the flesh. Venus—Lust, as it
were—envies this Soul; she sends Desire to destroy her; but because there is Desire for the Good as well as Desire for the Bad,
Desire loves Soul and mingles himself with her as if in union. He
persuades her not to see his face (that is, not to learn the bland-
ishments of desire—it's for this reason that Adam, even though
he sees, does not see that he is naked until he eats from the tree of
sexual desire), and not to give in to her sisters (that is, to Flesh
and Freedom) and so lose her life[9] by sticking her nose in as regards his shape and form. But she is terrified by their intimida-
tion and brings the oil lamp out from under the basket; that is, the
flame of desire that was hidden in her breast she brings out into
the open and, when she sees that it is as sweet as it is, she desires

---

7. "nothing but": retaining *tantum*, adverbial, for *tantam*, with Hays.

8. A corrupted name attributed to a doubtful source, but it does offer
some slender evidence that there were other treatments of a philosophical accounting of the relations of Cupid and Psyche.

9. Following Hays' emendation of *perdiscenda* to *peritura*.

it and loves it. And it is for this reason that she is said to have burned it by the boiling over of the lamp, because Desire always blazes up in proportion as it is loved and it impresses its sinful stain upon the flesh. Therefore, with Desire, as it were, stripped naked, Soul is deprived of her good fortune as mistress,[10] is tossed on a sea of perils, and is driven out of her royal residence. But because it is, as I've said, a lengthy business to pursue every detail, we have given just the general outline of the interpretation. On the other hand, all who read the tale itself in Apuleius will recognize for themselves, from the substance of our exposition, the remaining elements of which we have not spoken.

10. *potenti fortuna privatur:* the phrase is probably seriously corrupt.

Afterthoughts

A Matter of Plot

Understanding any story is a matter of retelling, of distilling from an array of detail some essential plot. In comparison to this extracted structure, which is meaningful in itself, the original story can be seen as one of a number of possible variations or elaborations. The story *Cupid and Psyche* is exceptionally rich and complex, but it does not resist such attempts at understanding; in fact, it encourages them and easily sponsors a large and wide range of interpretations, some complementary, some contradictory. *Cupid and Psyche* is a romance, or a folktale, or a Platonic allegory of the nature of the soul, or a Jungian tale of individuation, or an archetypal dream; the list may be extended. To say that it is all of these at once is dismissive of individual claims, while to say it is one and one only is naïve; to say that the story carried the author away, that it has a "life of its own," is similarly critically unsatisfying. But one can usefully concentrate on the word "plot." First, a reader needs to be able to extract a plot that does justice to as much detail as possible, one that accounts for the logic behind the story's complexities while bearing in mind that authors don't really write each story element as an iron-plated piece in some mechanically constructed allegory, even when they are writing allegories. Second, one needs to evaluate that plot against the demands of the themes involved and determine why such a theme is given such a treatment and whether propriety and consistency are relevant considerations.

The reader of the tale now knows just how difficult it is to summarize *Cupid and Psyche*. Partly this is a function of the extreme particularity of the details: what is it *like*, the fact that Psyche is carried down the cliff by the breath of the invisible West Wind or the fact that Psyche arranges to kill her sisters off by encouraging them to throw themselves into the arms of wind that will not be

there to receive them? Is Psyche a murderer? Is the story just getting rid of extraneous characters efficiently? Or are we witness-
ing some stage in the history or development of whatever it is
that Psyche *represents*? Partly it is a function of the author's own
inconsistencies. The lover is first imagined as invisible, as are all
the servants in the palace, yet Psyche can see him by lamplight;
she can feel his body and smell his hair and so knows his human
shape, yet her sisters convince her that he is a snake, and she
never managed to feel his wings and their feathers for all the
time that she embraced him. Is Psyche an idiot? Is the author just
engineering the dramatic visual scene of the revelation of Cupid
and so is indifferent to plot and plausibility? Or are we being
asked to consider what is the true nature of what Cupid *represents*? And then there is the problem of the shifting authorial
points of view. The robber's cook, a presumably illiterate old
woman, tells this elaborate tale, yet Apuleius at one point early
on (4.32) intrudes to say that Apollo delivered his oracle in Latin
out of deference to the author of the book. And since the oracle
speaks of Psyche as a bride of Death—a sacrifice to a snake-like
monster who tyrannizes both mortals and gods—and not, as
Venus had demanded, as a bride of some mortal wretch, has
Cupid been working behind the scenes, bribing Apollo as the
first step in his plan to have Psyche for himself, rewriting Venus'
commands? The author does not say. In fairy tales, motives, per-
sonalities, and the sequence of events can acquire a frustrating,
dream-like quality.

A further problem that makes the story difficult to summarize
is that it involves an oracle, gods, and the Underworld. Action
takes place on two different metaphysical, not just social, levels,
and leveling the two out in an attempt to find the fundamental
plot does some damage. Can Pan be reduced to just a wise old
man? The parents abandon Psyche because they believe that a
god has spoken to them. The sisters believe that their sister has
married a god, is pregnant with a god, and will become a god;
what were they thinking, then, when they instructed Psyche to
try to kill an immortal? The trip to the Underworld is literal and
real; the patriarch of the family is Jupiter himself. Two worlds col-
lide here, and the folktale storyline of the peasant girl improving
her social status by marrying the prince isn't a very satisfactory
parallel.

Here is an example of an inadequate reading, an extreme re-
duction that may serve as a cautionary tale. One could say that
Cupid and Psyche all boils down to the fundamental Hollywood
love story: boy meets girl (under extraordinary circumstances),
boy loses girl (through miscommunication), boy gets girl (and
both live happily ever after). This is not so much wrong as it is
trivializing. What is left out is the fact that the boy and the girl are
on two very different levels. Here is a fuller, and somewhat idio-
syncratic, retelling that I would offer as coming close to accounting for most of it, one that attempts to write out the gods:

A beautiful woman, no longer young, is horrified to discover that
everyone believes that some exceptionally beautiful young
woman is now her equal. She enlists her son to enact her scheme
for vengeance, but he, rather than trying to ensnare the young
woman in a marriage to some wretch of a man, falls in love with
her instead. In secret, without revealing his own identity to the
young woman or his actions to his mother, he arranges for an oracle to proclaim her to be the bride of Death; he then steals her
away when everyone thinks her dead, takes her to his palace, and
rapes her. He calls this love, for he makes her the mistress of his
palace and offers her everything that he has, adding the proviso
(presumably to keep his mother in the dark) that she must never
try to find out who he is, for he is invisible to her. The young
woman comes to accept the situation, believes herself to be fortunate and in love, and longs for her invisible husband's nightly re-
turnings. But she chafes at the restrictions and longs to see her
less fortunate older sisters, despite her husband's warnings that
they will ruin everything. The mysterious husband's youth, his
health, his wealth, his sexuality, all stand in contrast to the experiences of the sisters, married to old, ailing, miserly, sexless men.
The sisters, envious of the youngest sister's wealth and happiness, also have designs against this guileless young woman, trying to convince their youngest sister, now pregnant, that this
unknown husband is actually a monster, for they fear that he is
actually a god, that their child will be a god, and she will become
a goddess as well. They want her to kill her husband so that they
can take possession of her wealth and of her. She is oblivious to
their schemes and proves to be very tractable. She follows their
instructions. She brings a lamp in the night to see the sleeping
form of whatever it is that shares her bed and has a knife so that

she can kill it. He proves not to be a monster, and when she sees him in all his beauty, she does not use her knife but longs to embrace him all the more. Hot oil from her lamp scalds his shoulder and he awakes.

Though he had broken his mother's rules, he hypocritically punishes his beloved for breaking his rules. He abandons her, banishes her from his house, and so goes away, an immature whiner, back to his mother's house, to recuperate and to brood. The young woman, now resourceless and alone, attempts suicide in her weakness. Dissuaded from this, and encouraged by a wise old man to win her husband back by service, she becomes a wanderer. She finds her way, no one knows how, to the palaces of her sisters. Approaching them individually, she finds a curious courage. She lies and tells them that her husband wants to marry them instead. They individually try to win their way back to his palace, believing that his protection will let them survive the dangerous passage there, but their sister has her revenge. She has in fact engineered their doom and each falls to her death.

It is at this point that the mother finds out what her son has done and, in a towering rage, forbids her friends, otherwise sympathetic to the realities of youth and love, to help the young woman in any way at all. When the young woman meets these friends and begs for help, she is rebuffed and so decides to approach her mother-in-law directly for mercy. The mother-in-law proposes a series of tasks that she believes to be impossible, but the young woman receives unexpected help, accomplishes the increasingly deadly tasks, and so frustrates her taskmistress. She even manages the last task, a trip to the Underworld and back, but at the last moment, feeling that the mother-in-law is now out of the picture, she violates the prohibition that she was not to look into the jar that she was sent to fetch. Hoping to apply to herself a magic ointment, naïvely believing that she could become more beautiful and that her husband would appreciate any difference, she falls instead into the sleep of death, and it is at this point that her husband finally acts his age and comes to her rescue. He revives her and then sets about getting acceptance and approval for his marriage. Going over his mother's head, he appeals to the patriarch of the family, who gives his consent, wins the mother over to the state of affairs, and institutes a wedding celebration. Now, the patriarch jests, the young man will become a true husband, enjoying all the restrictions of domesticity. The mother, finally reconciled to becoming a grandmother, even dances at the wedding of her son. A child is born and everyone lives happily ever after.

And there you have it, three tales in one: a tale of the immature young man who is transformed from someone who has fallen in love with the mirror image of his mother to one who learns to stand up to his mother, whose love moves from what is private and secret to what is socially ordained; a tale of an immature and inexperienced young woman who learns the difference between rape and marriage, who grows up to discover that what shares her bed is not a monster but a man, who no longer lives in her parents' house but has found a new family, and is finally wife and mother; and a tale of a mother who learns with difficulty to accept the passing of time and to rejoice in the order of the generations and the inevitability of succession. It is the essential Comedy. The love that seems at first to break the social order asunder serves in fact to reestablish, reinvent, and reinvigorate it, and the wedding dance assures us that society has once again been made whole, blissfully incorporating the young into the world of the old. Delight has been born, not just to her parents, but for everyone.

Why isn't this a sufficient approach to Apuleius' *Cupid and Psyche*? As I said, it accounts for *most*, but not *all*. We start with the fairy-tale realm of social conventions and coming-of-age stories.[1] The pretty young woman comes up in the world; she rejects the family she grew up with in order to be accepted within her husband's family; her status as a married woman and mother leaves her anonymous parents alone in the recesses of their palace and her anonymous sisters dead. But we end up in the worlds of Soul and religion, and readers of the tale must grapple with them and wonder why a tale of a mortal soul's ascent to the realm of the immortal gods has been cast as a fairy tale. The oracle, the fear that the husband is a god, the trip to the Underworld: these cannot be written out of a synopsis, but they aren't the most important of the supernatural details, merely the most intractable. I would say that there are four main issues that must be addressed:

---

1. See now Anderson 2007, which I became aware of only as this book was going to press.

1. The young man's name is Cupid, and he is both the god of love and the boy with the bow and arrows. The young woman's name is Psyche, and this is the Greek word for Soul. The marriage takes place on Olympus after Jupiter literally offers Psyche the cup of immortality. This is not even allegory. On the simplest literal level, the story is about how Soul finds immortality through the intermediation of Love. This is therefore a philosophically as well as an erotically charged tale.

2. The mother-in-law is Venus, and she is described not only in comic terms as a woman who does not want to become a grandmother but also as an elemental force, the power behind the construction of the world at its beginning. The world whose order is at issue is not just social but universal. Further, the Love that is the engine of the Soul's immortality has been split in two, and Venus and Cupid are fundamentally at odds with each other, each displaying both comic and cosmic aspects: Cupid as whining boy and beautiful god, Venus as cosmic force and offended Roman matron. And at the end, Jupiter asserts the cosmic powers that Venus claimed for herself at the beginning (4.30, 6.22).

3. There is the long tradition of tales of Cupid and Psyche, extending well before this telling and known to us almost entirely through art, that must form part of the background of expectations in the readers who were the original audience. Not only do these traditions suggest a story of the Soul's ascent to immortality through Love, but they must have been stable enough for Plato to toy with them in *Phaedo* when he has Socrates describe how the experience of love (that is, the mature male's experience of nonprocreative love through his experience with a boy) is the first intimation of the soul's immortality and how the gooseflesh of the aroused lover suggests the feathers and wings that the lover needs in order to rise higher.

4. Why would the old woman who tells this tale, who has taken some cues from Charite's experiences and made *Cupid and Psyche* overlap the captive's tale in some crucial details, tell a story about the immature husband and the nasty mother-in-law? Why try to calm the fears of an abducted young woman with an account of how men and women both grow up? Why tell a tale that mixes miraculous escape and redemption through suffering?

How can one story inhabit the world of human society and its conventions and be at home as well among the immortals—immortals now grand, now trivial, comic, and inconsistent? The happy ending is also comic, with Jupiter joking about Psyche as Cupid's ball and chain and arranging for Cupid to continue to supply him with pretty, human girls—just because there are gods is no guarantee that the story is to be taken seriously. The example of Ovid's *Metamorphoses* is proof enough for Apuleius' *Metamorphoses*. And how can a story about Soul and Soul's return to heaven involve a Cupid who is so immature or involve a child born to the two of them that seems to represent the universal human emotion Delight? How can Cupid and Venus oppose each other in a philosophical allegory? The philosophical tradition, in evidence in Martianus Capella and Fulgentius as they try to explain *Cupid and Psyche* as allegory, has it that procreative sex is the process by which a soul descends into this world. Here we have an inversion by which heterosexual relations are the mechanism by which the soul may rise. For *Cupid and Psyche* within the philosophical tradition was never about procreative sex—this is Apuleius' innovation here, who follows the lead of more popular and sentimental treatments, presumably in art.

The Psychology of Romance

Taken as a whole, there is nothing like this story in ancient *literature* prior to Apuleius. It is hard to imagine, given how familiar the details sound, but he made up this particular concoction, compounding it largely out of story motifs available to him in mythology: three sisters, the bride of Death, the abandonment on a rock, the love affair between god and mortal, the rape, the suggestion of animal disguise, the fantastic palace that is the stock-in-trade of Ovid in *his Metamorphoses*, the trials set before the mortal before the mortal can become a god, and, of course, the iconographic and philosophical representations of Cupid and Psyche. It is quite a feat, but he is not inventing everything about this fantasy. There is a force that guides Apuleius here that is something other than philosophy but akin to folktale. The plot that underlies it is the romance plot, and to the extent that the romance is the popular mode for the narrative of experience (tragedy is the aristocratic one), it resembles the fairytale: a tale of separation, degradation, loss of identity reaching the extreme of loss of voice, living within the animal world, experiencing a symbolic death and then, in a blink-of-the-eye *peripeteia,* being restored to life, self, happiness and family through the ministrations of an ultimately benevolent deity who allows one to see that, in retrospect, all one's trials and sorrows were not meaningless but have been given meaning by the involvement of that deity. Providence appears explicitly in *Cupid and Psyche* at a couple of points. All of creation is conspiring in behalf of Psyche's success. Lucius' story in the frame is a romance, and so is Psyche's in the story itself; they reflect on each other.

Cupid and Psyche is told from the woman's point of view. I think that it is fundamentally what it seems on the surface to be: a frightening story about the passage from childhood to adulthood, about a maiden who, as she becomes a woman and a mother, learns that the thing that shares her bed is not a monster but a man. Certain Jungian elements are obvious, particularly in the talking animal helpers who get her through her tasks: the ants who help her sort the pile of seeds, the marsh reed that tells her how to gather the golden fleece of the bloodthirsty rams, the eagle that volunteers to fill Venus' bottle from the headwaters of the river Styx. For the journey to the Underworld, she must travel on her own two feet, but only after she receives detailed instructions from a tower that bursts into speech. This certainly counts as a journey of self-discovery, some sort of process of individuation, though it draws us up short at the end when Psyche shows how little she has learned. She opens the jar, falls into a coma, and is rescued by Cupid, who comes in at the end to save the day. Note that Psyche, after the death of her sisters, exhibits none of the cleverness that you may expect from a folktale heroine; as a woman, her virtues and vices, as revealed within the four trials to which Venus submits her, are expressed purely in terms of obedience and disobedience.

Even if the main character were not called Soul, you would still generalize from her experience toward some more universal statement about the relations between the sexes and about the nature of the individual in relation to the divinity that gives shape and meaning to human actions. Greeks and Romans do not have a psychological understanding of human nature; or, to put things more safely, they do not have a vocabulary of psychology, at least not until Augustine comes along and invents psychology. The romance tale of separation, loss of identity, and recovery of selfhood within the context of recovery of spouse and family is in fact one of the ways in which Greeks and Romans objectify the life of the mind and the soul. Journey and ordeal are the primary analogues for psychic development; thus, in late antiquity, the story of Odysseus is read in metaphysical terms as a tale of the life of the soul (its entry into this world, its return to its source), and these Neoplatonic readings of earlier epic are a significant impetus to the development of later epic (see Lamberton 1989).

So the Jungian analyst Erich Neumann overstates his case here and there in making *Cupid and Psyche* a story of the *psychic* development of the feminine (the woman has to be willing to kill within herself what is male, and then to be separate and independent from it, in order ultimately to be reunited with it and so to be whole), but he is not too far wrong; I would insist, however, that this theme isn't really unique to *Cupid and Psyche*. Where *Cupid and Psyche* becomes complex is in its blurring of the lines between the tale of the individual viewed as an independent and immutable entity—that is, the soul that has its origins in the eternal realm and seeks to return there—and the tale of a mutable person who matures within the social constructs of family and marriage. Allegorical readings invite us to view things the first way, psychological readings the second.[2]

The climactic scene, the revelation of Cupid, turns out to be something of a tease. Because the lover has been invisible, we have been purposely deprived of an opportunity to imagine the embrace of Cupid and Psyche, so crucial to their iconography, until Psyche pricks herself with the arrow and smothers him with kisses in his sleep (5.23). Psyche was the great beauty at the beginning of the story, but her beauty could not be put into words; consequently, we get a description of the beauty of Cupid instead as we turn our focus away from Psyche's physical attributes. Cupid was always the boy with the torch, yet he has no torch here (though it is referred to at 4.30, 4.31, and 5.29, it is strikingly

---

2. For a summary of Freudian and Jungian interpretations of the tale and its components, see the table taken from Gollnick (1992), at the end of this section.

absent from the weapons that Psyche sees at the foot of their bed at 5.22); Psyche with her lamp is substituted, and she plays the role of tormentor, burning his shoulder. This role reversal is quite appropriate for the romance, in which the couple comes to achieve what has been called a sexual symmetry (cf. Konstan 1993). Cupid pricked himself with his arrow, Psyche pricked herself, and each fell in love with the other. This revelation is the turning point of the story. They were joined as unequals; and at the point at which their essential equality is intimated, they separate so that they can reunite as equals and begin again. He will help her mature, to make the transition from daughter to wife; she will help him mature, so that at the end he is not the boy looking for his mother's image but the young man who can stop whining, take charge, and go over his mother's head to get approval for his marriage. But this evolution, so satisfactory to the extent that this is a love story and a romance, goes counter to the philosophical underpinnings that one is entitled to expect in any tale about Cupid and Psyche. This is, then, hardly a Platonic myth about Eros the intermediary, the demonic force that brings a soul back home, but a myth about human sexual love and its capacity to bring joy in this world while also providing an intimation of immortality in the next.

Psyche is surprised by Cupid's beauty, in particular by his wings. Her stunning naïveté not only reminds us that Psyche here has no wings but convicts Psyche of a most incredible obtuseness. She knew her lover's body inch by inch in the dark, its contours and its smells, the fall of Cupid's hair (5.13). How could she ever have been convinced that he was a snake of massive proportions and endless coils? And how could she have missed those wings? Psyche is simple, and simpleminded, when in the realm of Cupid, no longer the strong and self-willed daughter that she was when she was marching to her death. One of the reasons that Psyche is called simple is the folktale requirement that young women be naïve and helpless as they begin their journeys; but another is that the reader (if not the audience, the abducted bride Charite) knows all along who Psyche's husband is. This is a ridiculously prolonged dramatic irony. How long will it take her to find out what we knew from the minute we learned her name was Psyche? Cupid's invisibility is in fact a problem. We think that he is invisible because all of the servants in the palace are invisible, but it turns out that the room is just very dark, and a lamp is all that was ever needed. And what of the fact that all the interior walls of the palace are made of gold bricks and that all of the rooms, bedrooms included, shine with their own light regardless of whether it is day or night outside (5.1)? We could convict the old woman of sloppy storytelling if we wanted to; after all, Psyche could not have known and would not have guessed on her first inspection that the walls shone all day and all night; the omniscient narrator, trying to paint the scene for us, gets carried away, perhaps. Apuleius is in fact not that careful of an author. He has engineered a scene of great dramatic effect without giving much regard to its consistency or plausibility in detail. It seems that he takes a great visual interest in his narration; but his attention is spotty, and he visualizes a tableau much more satisfyingly than he does a sequence of actions. The intervention of the sisters, Cupid's repeated warnings, the speeches and the preparations— the whole sequence from 5.1 to 5.21—have nothing to do with philosophical allegory and everything to do with the drama of revelation and separation.[3]

And Cupid does not play the stern taskmaster. He abandons Psyche in a fit of pique, and she has to work out her salvation on her own. He plays the spoiled child, nursing a burned shoulder, while Psyche, attempting a mature response, is constantly talked out of suicide while trying to find a solution to her problem. She

---

3. A similar situation may be found in the events preceding *Cupid and Psyche*. In Book 3, The Festival of Laughter, Lucius is brought to trial for murder. The corpses of his three victims lie before the assembled crowd, covered with a cloth. We have four different accounts of the murder of these thugs who attempted to invade the house of Lucius' host Milo: Lucius himself is convinced that he did it, but that it was justifiable homicide. But it is an elaborate joke: the drunken Lucius slaughtered inflated goatskins that had been animated by a magic spell. The difficulties with this sequence of events are notorious, and one cannot arrive at a coherent explanation of how anyone planned the joke. But it all builds up to the drama of the revelation of the bodies at Lucius' trial. Lucius pulls back the cloth himself and expects to see the human corpses whose shapes are suggested by the drapery of that cloth; he sees instead the pierced goatskins. But this is the biggest problem: The goatskins are flat, pierced by Lucius' sword, so how could they seem to resemble the real, articulated, three-dimensional bodies of three men? The drama of the scene is foremost in the author's mind, the creation of the stunning tableau; plausibility, execution, and detail all take a back seat.

submits herself to the torments of Venus, who is playing here not a Heavenly or even a Vulgar Aphrodite but the nasty mother-in-law of fairy tales. Once *Cupid and Psyche* becomes *The Tale of the Mysterious Husband,* Venus has little choice but to play the witch. Now it is clear that Psyche is not constantly improving, and her yielding to the temptation to open Persephone's cosmetics jar shows just how little she has learned. Cupid swoops in to save her, but the closing scenes in heaven do not show him ushering her in. This is Jupiter's job. We are in the world of comedy. Conflict has to end in marriage; Venus has to be won over to the idea; Cupid gets Jupiter to override Venus' objections; Venus ends up dancing at her son's wedding. Jupiter offers Psyche the cup of immortality so that the wedding may be between social equals, and this will salve Venus' wounded pride. Jupiter wants Cupid married so that he'll have to stay at home and stop bothering the other gods; Psyche represents Cupid's ball and chain, though the price of Jupiter's acquiescence is that if Cupid does spot a really pretty mortal young woman he must make her known to Jupiter who, we presume, will continue his adulterous ways. It is hard to make this denouement fit an allegory of the Soul's progress. Cupid has proved to be not two Cupids but one Cupid compounded of two natures, and it is through his sexual relations with Psyche that he comes to be her equal, even as she becomes his.

The Structure of the Whole

The story in its original context is approximately one-quarter of the erotic and low-life *Golden Ass*. Its hero is a man who has been transformed into an ass because of a curiosity about magic. He too opens up a jar that he shouldn't have, which is why he becomes an ass. He too is a wanderer, subjected to increasing degradations, until he is saved by the goddess. The parallels between Psyche and Lucius, the ultimate narrator of *Cupid and Psyche* (he listened in as an ass when the old woman told it to the kidnapped maiden, and he tells it to us now that he is returned to his human shape and recalling his experiences from the tranquility of his salvation), are hardly exact, but they are numerous and substantial, and the reader of *Cupid and Psyche* first interprets it in the light of Lucius' prior transformation and then reinterprets it at the end of *The Golden Ass* after his salvation. We may ask whether Lucius-as-ass, overhearing *Cupid and Psyche*, brings to bear his own background as a student, as the nephew of the philosopher Plutarch. Of course he would know the philosophical traditions surrounding Cupid and Psyche. His reactions to the story, like those of Charite and the old woman, are of some interest. And he has a dismissive jingle for it—it is a *bella fabella*, a "beguiling fiction"—that does not suggest that he assigns a very great value to it himself.

It is often and inaccurately said to occupy the center of *The Golden Ass*, but *Cupid and Psyche* is approximately the second quarter of it, its end marking the midpoint of the story (pages 86–128 of the translation from which this is taken, marked as pages 3–254). Psyche's salvation and apotheosis on Olympus are to be compared and contrasted to Lucius' salvation through the intervention and the mysteries of Isis at the end of the whole. On the other hand, this tale is only part of a larger structure, the so-called Charite complex, which runs from the introduction of the abducted maiden to whom the tale is told to her death (pages 83–164); the tale of Charite can be said then to occupy the central third of *The Golden Ass*. Now Charite's tale is a tale of disaster. She tries to escape with the ass but is recaptured. Her salvation then seems to come in the person of her fiancé Tlepolemos, who infiltrates the robber band, makes himself captain, kills them all, and recovers his bride. All seems happy then back at home, but the evil Thrasyllus, a disappointed suitor, arranges to kill Tlepolemus while the two of them are out hunting and then attempts to seduce Charite. The bloody ghost of the husband appears to Charite in a dream and reveals all. She plots revenge, viciously blinds Thrasyllus and then kills herself. Finally, Thrasyllus shuts himself up in her tomb to starve himself to death. The old woman who tells *Cupid and Psyche* to Charite hopes to cheer her up and encourage her to believe, despite her abduction by robbers, that all will be well; but as far as Charite's life and experience are concerned, *Cupid and Psyche* is a pretty lie.

And the old woman who tells the story is playing on both sides of the fence. She works for the robbers who abducted Charite and is eager to see her richly ransomed. She doesn't want Charite to escape and will try hard to prevent it. She will kill herself when she fails. The content of the tale, be it the maturation of Psyche, or of Cupid, or of innocence rewarded, or of heaven achieved, is subordinate to its structure as a didactic fiction, as an old woman's story to calm a young woman's fears, *a story whose lesson will be proved wrong*. Charite's tale takes a long time to reach its dismal end; Psyche's story is no analogue to hers despite the initial similarities. The reader of the story may find it pretty and inspiring somehow or other, but subsequent events will chip away at it until it is completely hollowed out. The essence of romance is that, in retrospect, there is no meaningless coincidence, no mere luck that accounts for one's survival against all odds; the happy ending justifies the miserable means. But there is no happy ending for Charite, no god or goddess who watches over *her*.

The old woman says that dreams often mean the opposite of what they seem (4.27), and that ominous remark sets the tone for the Charite story and the function of *Cupid and Psyche* within it. Charite's nightmare was right, a dream of disaster; the old woman's fiction is the pious fraud. Now it seems to me that, in the event, the narrator does not find her personal story narrated in the tale that she told either; she sees no hope; she kills herself in despair, perhaps to save the robbers the trouble. Charite too will learn that this story has nothing to do with her. What Lucius the ass has learned from the story is the example of Psyche's courage. He says he will "wrap a man's courage around" himself and escape (6.26); this is what Psyche did in the story he just heard (5.22, 6.5), and Charite does the same (6.27; she will try to be a man again at 8.11 and 8.14 as she gathers strength for revenge and suicide). The ass and the maiden both escape and are recaptured; when they return to the robbers' camp they see that the old woman has hanged herself from a nearby tree (6.30). Their courageous actions avail them nothing; their lot is only improved when Charite's Prince Charming appears—her doomed Prince Charming—and they are taken away. As a moral lesson, *Cupid and Psyche* is a delusion.

Why such a cynical accounting? Here the answer is simple. Apuleius the author is now widely admired as a master of ambiguity, of false clues; we always wonder how he knows what he knows and who he is when he says it. He plays with the idea of the omniscient narrator; it remains unclear, and we believe purposefully, teasingly unclear, whether the speaker of the prologue of the whole is the same as the narrator; and when Lucius is

called the man from Madauros near the end (11.27; that's
Apuleius' hometown) the author seems to come to claim his character after he has been returned to his human shape. Are his tales
those of the experiencing ass or of the contemplative narrator?
There is a significant element of gamesmanship here. He always
leads us to believe something and then to disbelieve—or, if you
will, unbelieve—it. And at the beginning of *Cupid and Psyche* the
author sticks his nose into the old woman's narrative (4.32) to let
us know that he is really pulling the strings here.

Elaborate scenarios have been created whereby we see two
Venuses, corresponding to Plato's Heavenly Aphrodite and Vulgar Aphrodite, and two manifestations of Eros as well (Kenney
1990a and the introduction to Kenney 1990b). But why try to save
these phenomena? Why would we look for profundity in a tale
with these characters? Why would we think that characters simultaneously buffoons and cosmic principles can be hammered
into coherent allegory? When Apuleius takes the reader's expectations of the Heavenly and Vulgar Aphrodites and Eroses and
sets them loose in a domestic comedy about sexual maturation,
about the growth of Cupid and the birth of his child, he picks the
reader's pockets. We are looking for one sort of profundity and
getting another. And why should any story, as a story, be given
credence? It is surely telling that the three stories told before
Cupid and Psyche, three tales told by robbers and also overheard
by the ass, are of disastrous attempts at raiding expeditions in
which all the leaders are killed and most of the booty is lost; yet
they describe themselves as successes and their lost leaders as he-
roes. Their stories are exercises in self-deception. *Cupid and Psyche*
is a similar exercise. It expresses a truth about sex and the mortal
world, but its divine world is not held up for our admiration. The
tale's real concerns are those of the world below.

The Social and the Exceptional

If Psyche's tale is parallel to Lucius', one could say that Psyche's
tale has an unexpectedly comic ending, while Lucius' has an unexpectedly sublime one, by way of contrast. However that may
be, the comic ending—that is, its ending as a Comedy—of *Cupid*

and Psyche should not be taken as mere window dressing. Why put a comic ending to what had the potential for philosophical allegory? The answer is as simple as it is surprising. All of this wants to be universalizing. If Psyche is the psyche, everyone's soul, then the story is about how everyone has access through love to life eternal. But *The Golden Ass* is most emphatically not about that. For Lucius, sex was an element of his fall. When he is redeemed he is sexless, married, as it were, to Isis, but living a celibate life. Lucius' own story is closer to philosophical allegory than *Cupid and Psyche* is: sex is the process by which a noble soul is engendered and thus lost in this world, and the return of the soul, and Lucius' return, involves a rejection of sex.[4] And if Psyche is everyone's soul, then the immortality made available to her is available to everyone; but at the end, Lucius, who has been expensively initiated three times, twice into the mysteries of Isis and finally into those of Osiris, is promised a bliss in the next world that is not available to all, but to the special few.

And, perhaps most important, the Isis who saves Lucius is a goddess without a story. *Cupid and Psyche* is a tale of comic Olympian gods, and of gods behaving badly. Why would anyone look to this Venus, this Cupid, this Jupiter, for truth or consolation? It is the very fact that they are characters in a story that convicts them of triviality and irrelevance. When Lucius is claimed by Isis, we hear nothing of the stories we know elsewhere about Isis, Osiris, Horus, and Seth: no mournful wife collecting the pieces of her dead and dismembered husband; no battle between brothers, or between forces of Light and Darkness. Isis saves Lucius despite himself, not because he has earned it; and he is not saved through sex and marriage. That great folktale motif, that of the monster turned into a civilized man through the love of a woman (and which is richly attested in medieval Latin tales, particularly the Latin *Asinarius*), is explicitly rejected in the frame story. Lucius the ass will not sleep with the condemned woman, though he had slept with a peculiarly oversexed Roman matron who left him unchanged; transformation is not part and parcel of love. Truth is outside of story and fiction. In terms of religion, it is

4. Similarly, the massive frame story in Martianus Capella's *Marriage of Philology and Mercury* (see Appendix II) is truer to the philosophical traditions concerning Cupid and Psyche than the allegorization of Apuleius' treatment of it that Martianus presents in his opening pages.

folly to look to Olympian gods for truth; they are comic relief compared to the august Isis. Lucius' spiritual devotion to his goddess is not like Psyche's sexual devotion to Cupid; it is a tale of immortality achieved in both cases, but Lucius' transformation and salvation are *real*.

At the end of Book 10, Lucius the ass escapes from a theater at Corinth and will then have his vision of Isis on the beach at Cenchreae. He was waiting to be put on display in a donkey show, a fate that horrified him. What he is watching while in the wings is an elaborate mime production of the Judgment of Paris. This too is a tale of Venus, who wins her beauty contest with Juno and Minerva by bribing Paris with Helen and so precipitating the Trojan War. This is not cosmic Venus; this is another Venus from which Lucius runs away. The stories of classical mythology are always warnings to Lucius, as becomes clearer to him in the course of the romance. The statue of the fate of Actaeon that he sees in Book 2 does not teach him to be careful about curiosity; the story of Cupid and Psyche inspires him to bravery, but not to immortality; with the Judgment of Paris, enough is enough. He escapes from the world of myth and story and finds salvation in the imperious love of Isis, the goddess without a story. It is at this point that we see Apuleius the author in his true Platonic colors. What is ultimately true is not a fit subject for words and discursive thought. Isis is true because she is not a story; the Olympian gods are stories, and Lucius' salvation does not lie there. And Lucius' story, when it resumes after *Cupid and Psyche,* is designed to show how his path and those of both Psyche and Charite differ utterly. *Cupid and Psyche* will for him represent the path not taken.

So now we can come back inside *Cupid and Psyche* after looking outside of it. It is a love story, set in a larger tale that makes sex a part of the hero's degradation. It is a tale of love between man and woman, leading to the birth of a child, and thus at odds with the reader's philosophical expectations. It shows the restoration of society, set in a larger tale that ends with the narrator living as a willing outsider. The old woman tells it to Charite to encourage her to believe that both her life and her society will be restored and that the gods are looking out for her. These gods will be shown to have no value outside of the story, but the influence of the tale can be attributed to its refusal to be truly a philosophical allegory. A man and a woman, love, sex, a child—all parts of a tale of immortality achieved; a story of the equality of man and woman; a story of maturity within the real world, leading to a blissful life here and a conviction of bliss in the world beyond. It is not about the fall of the soul, or of its sinful nature, or its need to return by itself through the intermediation of a demonic spirit; that is what *The Golden Ass* is about. *The Golden Ass* is what *Cupid and Psyche* would have been about if it followed the expectations imposed upon it by the philosophical tradition. *Cupid and Psyche* does indeed form an index by which to judge the whole of the romance, but the key term is *contrast*. A society restored by the sexual maturity and fruition of a man and a woman is what appeals most to readers at various times and to imitators in various media. Sex is next to godliness. But to Lucius, it is a parody of truth; to Apuleius, Platonic storyteller, it is a story that, by virtue of its being a story, has no claim on philosophical truth. To the extent that a virtuoso storyteller can, *The Golden Ass* locates truth in a world beyond story. *Cupid and Psyche* is merely a blissful diversion, offering to the reader an ecstatic account of how heterosexual experience within the real and social world offers a proof of the life divine, where human desire changes the nature of divine love, and where all trial leads to a bliss that is heaven on earth. The world into which the immortal Psyche gains access is an image of this world; the ultimate divine realities lie elsewhere.

Table 1: *Psychological Interpretations of the Eros and Psyche Myth*

From James Gollnick. *Love and the Soul.* Waterloo, Ontario: Wilfrid Laurier University Press, 1992, 114–5.

Author	Story symbolizes	Psyche	Eros	Aphrodite	Sisters	Voluptas	Tasks
Freudian Interpretations							
Riklin 1908	a psychotic's wishfulfillment	psychotic's mind	a hallucinating wishfulfillment	persecutor	figures in contrast to hero	—	life difficulties; escape hallucination
Schroeder 1917	a girl's erotic dream	a girl	man; penis' monster	—	—	—	—
Barchilon 1959	an adolescent girl's anxieties	an adolescent girl	man; father; sex as beastly	—	sexual anxieties	—	—
Bettelheim 1976	a woman's reaching for consciousness	a woman; rational soul	sexuality	regressive form of sexuality	sexual anxiety	—	process of overcoming sexual anxiety
Hoevels 1979	a woman's Oedipal fantasy	a woman	man; penis; father-substitute; serpent	rival mother; object of Psyche's death wish	sibling rivals; objects of Psyche's death wishes	—	working out the guilt due to death wishes

Jungian Interpretations

Neumann 1956	female development	woman (ego, total psyche, an archetype)	eros within the psyche; paternal *uroboros*; man	unconscious; bad mother archetype	matriarchal stratum in the psyche, Psyche's shadow	mystical joy	aspects (stages) of female's development
von Franz 1970	anima development	Apuleius' (and Lucius') anima	animus; *puer aeternus* aspect of self archetype	unconscious; mother archetype	self-preservative instinct	sensual lust	aspects of anima's development
Ulanov 1971	anima development	anima	drive to involvement; archetype of deity	unconscious; mother archetype	neglected, un-differentiated feminine elements	symbol of self archetype	stages of anima's development
Hillman 1972	soul-making; psychological creativity	anima (becoming psyche)	masculine creative principle; daimon linking gods to humans	fecundity; promiscuity; emotionality	—	pleasure of creativity	aspects of soul-making
Johnson 1976	female and anima development	woman and man's anima	man; woman's animus; *puer aeternus*; God-archetype	unconscious; mother archetype or complex	Psyche's shadow	joy or ecstasy	aspects of inner development
Houston 1987	female and anima development	woman and man's anima	drive toward development and expression; psycho-pomp linking personal self to beyond	unconscious; unreflected archetypes	doubts arising from a one-sided situation	source of instinct, wisdom and culture	psychological ordeals in search of completion

Bibliography

Accardo, Pasquale. *The Metamorphosis of Apuleius. Cupid and Psyche, Beauty and the Beast, King Kong*. Madison, WI, and Teaneck, NJ: Fairleigh Dickinson University Press, 2002.

Anderson, Graham. *Folktale as a Source of Greco-Roman Fiction: The Origin of Popular Narrative*. Lewiston, NY: Edwin Mellen Press, 2007.

Barchilon, Jacques. "Beauty and the Beast: From Myth to Fairy Tale." *Psychoanalysis and the Psychoanalytic Review* 46.4 (1959): 19–29.

Bettleheim, Bruno. *The Uses of Enchantment: The Meaning and Importance of Fairy Tales*. New York: Knopf, 1976.

Calder, William M., III, Bernhard Huss, Marc Mastrangelo, R. Scott Smith, and Stephen M. Trzaskoma, trans. *The Unknown Socrates*. Wauconda, IL: Bolchazy-Carducci Publishers, 2002.

Carver, Robert H. F. *The Protean Ass: The* Metamorphoses *of Apuleius from Antiquity to the Renaissance*. Oxford Classical Monographs. Oxford: Oxford University Press, 2007.

Cavicchioli, Sonia. *The Tale of Cupid and Psyche: An Illustrated History*. Translated by Susan Scott. New York: George Braziller, 2002.

Cooper, John M., ed. *Plato: Complete Works*. Indianapolis: Hackett Publishing Co., 1997.

Dillon, John. *The Middle Platonists*. 2nd ed. Ithaca, NY: Cornell University Press, 1996.

Gaisser, Julia Haig. *The Fortunes of Apuleius and the* Golden Ass: *A Study in Transmission and Reception*. Princeton, NJ: Princeton University Press, 2008.

Gersh, Stephen. *Middle Platonism and Neoplatonism: The Latin Tradition*. Vol. I. Notre Dame, IN: University of Notre Dame Press, 1986.

Gollnick, James. *Love and the Soul: Psychological Interpretations of the Eros and Psyche Myth*. Editions SR, Vol. 15. Waterloo, Ontario: Wilfrid Laurier University Press, 1992.

———. *The Religious Dreamworld of Apuleius'* Metamorphoses: *Recovering a Forgotten Hermeneutic*. Editions SR, Vol. 25. Waterloo, Ontario: Wilfrid Laurier University Press, 1999.

Harrison, Stephen, John Hilton, and Vincent Hunink, trans. *Apuleius: Rhetorical Works*. Oxford: Oxford University Press, 2001.

Hays, Bradford Gregory. "Fulgentius the Mythographer." Ph.D. diss., Cornell University, 1996.

Helm, Rudolf. *Apulei Platonici Madaurensis Opera Quae Supersunt*. Vol. I, *Metamorphoseon Libri XI*. 3rd ed. Reprint with addenda, 1968. Leipzig, Germany: Teubner, 1931.

———, ed. *Fabii Planciadis Fulgentii V.C. Opera. . . .* Reprint of the 1898 edition, with addenda by J. Préaux. Stuttgart, Germany: Teubner, 1970.

Hijmans, B. L., Jr., R. Th. van der Paardt, E. R. Smits, R. E. H. Westendorp Boerma, and A. G. Westerbrink. *Apuleius Madaurensis Metamorphoses*. Book IV 1–27: *Text, Introduction, and Commentary*. Groningen Commentaries on Apuleius. Groningen, The Netherlands: Egbert Forsten, 1977.

Hijmans, B. L., Jr., R. Th. van der Paardt, V. Schmidt, R. E. H. Westendorp Boerma, and A. G. Westerbrink. *Apuleius Madaurensis Metamorphoses*. Books VI 25–32 and VII: *Text, Introduction, and Commentary*. Groningen Commentaries on Apuleius. Groningen, The Netherlands: Egbert Forsten, 1981.

Hijmans, Benjamin Lodewijk, and Rudolf Theodor van der Paardt, eds. *Aspects of Apuleius' Golden Ass*. Vol. II: *Cupid and Psyche*. Groningen, The Netherlands: Bouma's Boekhuis, 1998.

Hillman, James. *The Myth of Analysis: Three Essays in Archetypal Psychology*. Evanston: Northwestern University Press, 1972.

Hoevels, Fritz Erik. *Märchen und Magie in den* Metamorphosen *des Apuleius von Madaura*. Amsterdam: Rodopi, 1979.

Hofmann, Heinz, ed. *Latin Fiction: The Latin Novel in Context*. London and New York: Routledge, 1999.

Houston, Jean. *The Search for the Beloved: Journeys in Sacred Theology*. Los Angeles: J. P. Tarcher, 1987. ["Psyche and Eros," pp. 151–88.]

Johnson. R. *She: Understanding Feminine Psychology: An Interpretation Based on the Myth of Amor and Psyche and Using Jungian Psychological Concepts*. New York: Harper and Row, 1976.

Kenney, E. J. "Psyche and Her Mysterious Husband." In *Antonine Literature*, edited by D. A. Russell, 175–98. Oxford: Oxford University Press, 1990a.

———, ed. *Apuleius: Cupid and Psyche*. Cambridge: Cambridge University Press, 1990b.

Konstan, David. *Sexual Symmetry: Love in the Ancient Novel and Related Genres*. Princeton, NJ: Princeton University Press, 1993.

Lamberton, Robert. *Homer the Theologian: Neoplatonist Allegorical Reading and the Growth of the Epic Tradition*. Transformation of the Classical Heritage. Berkeley: University of California Press, 1989.

Lev Kenaan, Vered. "Delusion and Dream in Apuleius' *Metamorphoses*." *Classical Antiquity* 23 (2004): 247–84.

Lewis, C. S. *Till We Have Faces: A Myth Retold*. San Diego and New York: Harcourt Brace and Company, 1956.

Moreschini, Claudio, ed. *Apulei Opera Philosophica*. Stuttgart, Germany: Teubner, 1991.

Myers, Doris T. *Bareface: A Guide to C. S. Lewis' Last Novel*. Columbia: University of Missouri Press, 2004.

Neumann, Erich. *Amor and Psyche: The Psychic Development of the Feminine, A Commentary on the Tale by Apuleius*. Translated by Ralph Manheim. Bollingen Series LIV. Princeton, NJ: Princeton University Press, 1956.

O'Brien, Elmer, trans. *The Essential Plotinus: Representative Treatises from the Enneads*. Reprinted 1975 from the 1964 edition. Indianapolis: Hackett Publishing Co.

O'Brien, Maeve C. *Apuleius' Debt to Plato in the* Metamorphoses. Lewiston, NY: Edwin Mellen Press, 2002.

Partridge, John. "Socrates, Rationality, and the Daimonion." *Ancient Philosophy* 28 (2008): 1–25.

Penwill, J. L. "Reflections on a 'Happy Ending': The Case of Cupid and Psyche." *Ramus* 27 (1998): 160–82.

Pepin, Ronald E., trans. *The Vatican Mythographers*. New York: Fordham University Press, 2008.

Reid, Jane Davidson. *The Oxford Guide to Classsical Mythology in the Arts*. Oxford: Oxford University Press, 1993. [Eros, v.1 391–421; Psyche, v.2 939–55.]

Relihan, Joel C. *Ancient Menippean Satire*. Baltimore, MD: Johns Hopkins University Press, 1993.

———, trans. *Apuleius: The Golden Ass or, A Book of Changes*. Indianapolis: Hackett Publishing Co., 2007.

Riklin, Franz. *Wunscherfüllung und Symbolik im Märchen.* Vienna and Leipzig: Franz Deutike, 1908. Translated by William A. White. *Wishfulfillment and Symbolism in Fairy Tales.* New York: The Nervous and Mental Disease Publishing Company, 1915. Reprint New York: Johnson Reprint Corp., 1970.

Rist, John M. "Plotinus and the 'Daimonion' of Socrates." *Phoenix* 17 (1963): 13–24.

Schlam, Carl. *Cupid and Psyche: Apuleius and the Monuments.* University Park, PA: The American Philological Association, 1976.

———. *The* Metamorphoses *of Apuleius: On Making an Ass of Oneself.* Chapel Hill: University of North Carolina Press, 1992.

Schlam, Carl, and Ellen Finkelpearl. "A Review of Scholarship on Apuleius' *Metamorphoses* 1970–1998." *Lustrum* 42 (2000): 7–223.

Schroeder, J. A. *Het Sprookje van Amor en Psyche in het Licht der Psychoanalyse.* Baarn, The Netherlands: Hollandia, 1917.

Scobie, Alex. *Apuleius and Folklore: Toward a History of ML3045, AaTh567, 449A.* London: The Folklore Society, 1983.

Shanzer, Danuta. *A Philosophical and Literary Commentary on Martianus Capella's* De Nuptiis Philologiae et Mercurii, Book 1. Classical Studies, Vol. 32. Berkeley: University of California Press, 1986.

Shumate, Nancy. *Crisis and Conversion in Apuleius'* Metamorphoses. Ann Arbor: University of Michigan Press, 1996.

Stahl, William Harris, Richard Johnson, and E. L. Burge. *Martianus Capella and the Seven Liberal Arts,* Vol. I. Records of Civilization: Sources and Studies, Number 84. New York: Columbia University Press, 1971.

———, trans. *Martianus Capella and the Seven Liberal Arts,* Vol. II: *The Marriage of Philology and Mercury.* Records of Civilization: Sources and Studies, Number 84. New York: Columbia University Press, 1977.

Ulanov, Ann Belford. *The Feminine in Jungian Psychology and in Christian Theology.* Evanston: Northwestern University Press, 1971.

von Franz, Marie-Louise. *The Golden Ass of Apuleius: The Liberation of the Feminine in Man.* Revised 1992. Boston and London: Shambhala Press, 1970.

Willis, James, ed. *Martianus Capella.* Leipzig, Germany: Teubner, 1983.

Winkler, John J. *Auctor & Actor: A Narratological Reading of Apuleius's* Golden Ass. Berkeley: University of California Press, 1985.

Zimmerman, M., S. Panayotakis, V. C. Hunink, W. H. Keulen, S. J. Harrison, Th. D. McCreight, B. Wesseling, and D. van Mal-Maeder. *Apuleius Madaurensis Metamorphoses*. Books IV 28–35, V, VI 1–24, *The Tale of Cupid and Psyche. Text, Introduction, and Commentary*. Groningen Commentaries on Apuleius. Groningen, The Netherlands: Egbert Forsten, 2004.

Ziolkowski, Jan M. *Fairy Tales from Before Fairy Tales: The Medieval Latin Past of Wonderful Lies*. Ann Arbor: University of Michigan Press, 2007.

Index

This index is a condensation of the index prepared for the printed translation of the entire *Golden Ass*; the reader is referred to the online index (available at www.hackettpublishing.com), which is fuller still. Comparison of the two may prove instructive for readers contemplating the particularities of the action and the atmosphere of *Cupid and Psyche*. Not only are there the predictable differences (there are no magistrates, no priests, no soldiers, no witches in *Cupid and Psyche*) but also there are many surprises: there is no blushing, no cooking, no dramatic metaphors, no Egyptian divinities, nothing left-handed, no oaths, no Odysseus, no rags, no rocks and stones, no seasons, and, while there is sunrise, there is no Sun. On the other hand, certain key terms make their presence felt both within and without *Cupid and Psyche* (sadism/sadistic, salvation/salvific/savior, sticking one's nose in), and here the comparison of the two indexes will reveal the continuity of themes between this story and its frame. Materials in the Appendix are not included.